Secrets of Sweettooth

Tiamo Pastoor

A playful story from the Handheld Disk

(Book #5)

COPYRIGHT

CONTENTS

"Don't ▮▮▮▮ the player from
▮▮▮▮▮▮ Give meaningful
▮▮▮▮ then ▮▮▮▮ the fun."

4

Δ Chance at Friendship

Surely the Memory Police did not intend to turn me into an awkward piece of *candy*. That doesn't make it any less true.

Being a candy has the added downside of lacking limbs. And I like having limbs, thank you very much. I have eyes, and ears, probably an entire face. It allows me to look at my form—a wrapped red toffee—but I struggle to even rotate.

"Hello? Memory Police? Where's my favorite giant crab?" I ask. "A bit of help?"

I can still hear their grumpy voice, the clattering of corks and keys from their belt as they walk. But they sound far away. Dull. Out of reach.

What kind of game *is* this?

I look ahead. We're on a tropical island, where a soft breeze ruffles my plastic wrapper and bends palm trees. A pirate ship floats in the distance and parrots circle overhead. Not exactly a candyland.

I can feel some floor beneath me, but it doesn't feel like sand.

Then I look down—and I shouldn't have.

I'm not standing on the beach. I'm standing at the top of a tall, tall stack of other objects.

A few candies, though a different type. Some fishes in different colors and sizes. Some golden coins, squashed palm trees, and a nice treasure chest at the base. All of us are exactly the same square dimensions and placed in a perfect stack, more like … like a column in a grid.

"Wildebyte! Where are you, troublemaker?" the Memory Police grunts, the dullness leaving their voice.

If I can't rotate, then maybe I can look around some other way.

I strain to push my eyes sideways. My peripheral vision only shows more and more of these stacks, all the same height, but filled with wildly different items. No matter how long I study them, I can only find *one* item that appears more than once: the cute parrot.

The Camera enters my view. A black shiny box, hanging from the sky using a thick electrical cord. The moment I enter its view I am forced to follow the game's code.

The Player swipes across me. In the real world, it's probably just their fingertip moving an inch across their phone's screen. In here, a floating finger nudges me to the side and leaves a trail of tiny sparkling stars.

I *swap* places with a wooden barrel next to me. My only reward is a deafeningly loud and sad error sound. The action failed; we swap back.

The Player tries two more times, until they find the parrot. The one thing that actually exists multiple times. They place the three of them in a nice row.

This time, their reward is a loud and happy sound, including some confetti that splatters across my face. Great. Great for them. Now get me out of here.

Unfortunately, the real reward is *more points* and the parrots *disappearing* from underneath me. As soon as the gap is created, the entire part of the stack above it falls down. That includes me. Now I can study the grains of sand from a closer distance.

A *flying ship* passes overhead in a hurry. When they reach my stack, they drop a new item on top of my head. Or, well, on top of my entire toffee body, which is also my head. All gaps are quickly filled and the Camera zooms to a new location, inviting the Player to take their next turn.

The ship seems to refill the levels. At it flies on, I catch its very creative name written in bold letters: *Level Ship*.

Did I already mention how awful this experience is?

I thought my previous games were bad. Now I long for the days when I actually had the shape of an animal and could walk, talk, and act freely.

Once the freshness of the new game wears off, that's all that remains: longing for a better place. Missing the rare friends I made in the previous games. How would Lulu be doing? Would she miss me just as much? Sometimes I can feel her tugging at some code inside me, and I don't know whether to be happy or feel even more lonely.

All of them couldn't come with me, because I seem to be the only one who can walk between games. Well, except for—

A smiling pirate emerges from the crystal-clear waves. Soaking wet, he arrives on the beach. Miniature versions of many in-game items dance around him attached to ropes and chains.

"Aye! Player finally be making smart-skulled moves. Soon they be ready for the harrrrder levels."

"Pirate Sweettooth!" I yell.

I laugh. Hope swells in my heart.

His hand still has a hole where his sword should be. Cookie crumbs are visible on his clothing like sticky glitters impossible to get rid off.

"I'm here! Wildebyte!"

The Player creates another match. Not that hard when there's only *one* item that appears multiple times. But hey, if they're happy, I'm happy.

"Can you hear me?" I yell even louder. The Camera turns back to me, which forces me to shut up and look like an innocent little toffee.

I can't see what happens. All I hear is a rough grinding sound, several times in a row, as if Sweettooth is *dragging* himself towards me. At least, I hope so, because the sound gets louder, and I haven't felt this hopeful in a while.

When the Camera finally leaves, Sweettooth is *right in my face.*

"Wildebyte! You be an unpredictable fellow, aye." He winks. "Orrr a sweetie, I guess."

Then his face pulls taut, as if suddenly remembering his ship is on fire.

He is now part of the stacks. The beach doesn't show any footprints, nor have I actually seen him walk. A sneaky suspicision washes over me.

"Even *you* can't walk in your own game?"

He shakes his head. "We only be moving by swapping with something else."

He leans his body to the side. Behind him is a long row of displaced objects, including palm trees suddenly upside down in the ocean and a few parrots living underneath a rock.

Something taps my shoulder from the other side. The Memory Police. They *don't* have to follow all the rules in the game. I'm not jealous, you are jealous.

"My apologies for the mistake." They sound sincere. Didn't know they could. "This game is such a mess that even I can't figure it out. I'll put you in another game, one with just a single humanoid character and nothing else!"

They already assume I will go along, forcefully dragging me out of the stack of candy. The items above me yelp as they unexpectedly fall down. To make matters worse, the new item dropped at the top is an entire *ship*.

And, yes, I know what I just said. Normally I would leave an awful game like this in a heartbeat.

But another game where I'll be alone ...

But Sweettooth is right here ...

Finally freed from the stack, I can at least *rotate* freely. The Camera is leaving as the Player loses their interest, scoring a mediocre highscore on ... level 1.

I look Sweettooth in the eyes. "You can Gamewalk. I've seen you in multiple games now."

"Aye! But this be my home, that it be."

"How?"

The Memory Police grows impatient. "Let's go, troublemaker. I have hundreds of rogue apps and games to keep in line, can't wait on you."

Sweettooth doesn't answer and walks away. Or, rather, *swaps* away.

The scene before me turns into *chaos*. Everything swaps with everything, shifting around as if tourists overwhelmed the beach. Messy tourists who don't understand the local customs nor speak each other's language. Panicked tourists who need to swap places with a tree, a rock, or a barrel just to move around.

Sweettooth disappears among them. He—again—gives the impression that he realized something is on fire.

I wriggle out of the Police's grasp. "No. I'm staying!"

"Sure?" they grunt. "I'm not coming back for you."

I already touch the beach to look at the code inside. To figure out how to get myself to swap.

"I … I am sure. A hundred and twenty percent. Surest as surely can be."

"Doesn't sound sure."

The giant orange crab shrugs and turn around, using some invisible exit I can't find. They just vanish. So much for leaving this game any time soon.

But it was the right decision. It has to be. No more loneliness. If I can't share my joy with others, then what's the point? And I'm slowly losing hope that I'll find my way out of Ludra, back to my real life, on my own.

I steady myself and focus on reaching Sweettooth before they sail away.

Okay. Ready to do my first swap with that palm tree next to me. Ready to—an error sound plays, limited to my own ears, as my toffee body feels like it hits a brick wall.

That's when I learn that the *other* item has to agree to do the swap. And they aren't eager to help the infamous Wildebyte.

Not For Sweethaven

Surprisingly, talking to a brick wall is like talking to a brick wall. All items in this game have a face and can communicate, even the palm trees and treasure chests, but they just don't say anything useful.

"Please," I plead. "Sweettooth is getting away. Swap? Please?"

"No. You're the Wildebyte."

"Yes. So it would be an *honor* to swap with me!"

"I don't trust you."

"Argh!"

All this time, I apparently stood on top of some golden coins. Once they swap away from me, I fall down into the gap below. This means I can have this conversation *again* with a lollipop candy.

The developers of this game were truly insane when they coded this. Who thought to combine candy, jewelry and pirates into a single game? And turn them all into characters with faces?

Sweettooth is just a blip on the horizon, looking for the next object to swap with. The sun sets, lengthening the shadows from the palm trees and turning the horizon into waves of black silhouettes.

"What do you *want*?" I yell at the lollipop. Their face is cute and cartoony, and their voice that of a baby.

"What all items in Pirate Pound want."

Pirate Pound? I thought Sweettooth's game was called Sugar Stomp. This is just more proof that he *can* Gamewalk.

"And that is?" I press impatiently.

"To find our perfect match and go to Sweethaven!"

I look around. Now that the Player isn't playing, the game isn't confined to showing what's inside the level. Many more items have come out of the woodworks—or should I say *sandworks*—and there are way more duplicates.

The Level Ship that refilled the stacks acts like a taxi, picking up items when they're stuck and unswappable, to drop them off where they wanted to be. It's seemingly the only thing that can move in a normal way. Well, if you call a flying ship *normal*.

I could ask those other lollipops to come here. It would take time and convincing. My adventures in the previous game gave me a tiny bit of Data Doubloons—money in Ludra—but surely not enough to bribe all of them.

"I don't have time for this!"

Sweettooth disappears in the distance. I grab the lollipop and reach inside their code. They gasp and look at me as if I ripped off their clothes in public.

Ah. There. Two numbers, x and y, that determine their location in this world. They are now standing at (3,6)—column 3, row 6. This means I must be at (2,6)—column 2, row 6.

I forcefully change the numbers to move the lollipop to *my* current location. This prompts the game world to swap us by default. It probably can't handle two things in the same spot.

"*Outrageous!*" the lollipop yells, pointing their stick at me like a sword. They turn to the other items for support. "Did you see what that toffee did? The *audacity!*"

They all nod and eagerly try to swap away from me.

"Sweethaven will forever be closed to you, Wildebyte!"

I ignore their cries and force a palm tree to swap with me, then a coin, then a sword, then a treasure chest, faster and faster, before they can flee out of my reach.

Matching the speed of the Level Ship overhead, I rapidly crest the sand dunes and find Sweettooth *digging* into a different part of the beach.

Ah. Of course. Looking for treasures on his own island. Real smart.

"Sweettooth! I figured out your game."

"Did you know, aye?" he says without looking up. "I've already received fifty complaints from my items."

"They wouldn't help me."

"And so you be forcing them to do what you want?"

This isn't going well. I perform my last swap, with a fish swimming through the beach as if they were still underwater, and then I'm pressed right up against him.

"I'm sorry. But I'm here now. We can Gamewalk together! We can help each other! You must have seen my Lost Memory around here, right?"

Sweettooth turns to me, his face dark and grim. "And what makes you think I be wanting to travel with *you*?"

"I ... I ... " My voice shrinks to its smallest form. "Why not?"

"You're a dark demon! You be ruining every game you enter and, aye, too powerful to control."

How do I convince him? What do I say? And why does he keep digging in random places?

"I'll prove it to you! What are you searching for? I'll help you find it, right now."

He just shakes his head. "Not a feather on my parrot who'd work with you."

"You don't have a parrot."

"It be an expression."

He swaps places with that same fish to get away from me, then finds a forest of palm trees to flee even more quickly. I struggle to follow, *forcing* them all to swap with me.

"So that's it?!" I yell, my voice shrill and panicked. My toffee body starts to unwrap itself. "You just … you just hate me so much?"

"It be harrrd to convince the Guild," he mutters. Then he freezes, face blank. Yes, I've heard that word before.

"Guild? You know about the Guild? What are they?"

"No no! We don't be speaking a word about the Guild, aye!" They regain composure. "And also, yes, I bottom-barrel hate you. Not even Sweethaven could convince me to touch the Wildebyte!"

Rage rumbles inside my sweet belly. I want to kick, scream, grab Sweettooth and force their code to travel with me. That's all they are!

"You're just pieces of code!" I scream. "I don't need you. You just follow patterns and commands. You do whatever some rules in your brain tell you to do. Your emotions are programmed. Some rule in your brain says that if an entity threatens your game, you're supposed to hate them. Yes! That's all you are!"

He takes off his pirate hat and looks at me like a worried father. "Oh? Then what are *you*?"

"I am *different*. I am *better*."

"I be thinking I made the right choice," he mumbles as he leaves me alone on the beach.

All my energy leaves me. What's the point? The only person that could share my adventures looks like they want to kill me.

And still I feel, as clearly as I yearn to see my parents again, that we could be the greatest match of all time. Two powerful Gamewalkers, together.

So I make a final attempt. "Let me prove it to you! Give me a mission. Give me your *rules* that would make you stop hating me!"

Sweettooth points at a small ship. Its sharp point is driven into the beach, as if its sailors had too much speed and couldn't brake before reaching the island. The pirate is mostly interested in two counters: big, blocky numbers punched into the side.

"The Player barely be playing us and too empty-skulled to finish even level 1! If we get uninstalled ..."

No need to finish that sentence. In Ludra, *uninstall* is just a different word for *death*. Being erased as if you never existed.

Sweettooth continues. "The Guild—I mean, this lovely Pirate here—would ask you to be fixing the game and get it played, aye. Get everyone to like you and that be a first step."

He still watches me with grim eyes. "That be a first step of many, many steps."

The other counter is still at zero. I wonder what that's for, but don't dare ask now.

"I accept! I accept."

Until suddenly all the grinding noises, all the chittering and swapping from items across the island, *stops* all at once.

"Arrr! You made me too slow! See what you do?!"

He furiously searches underneath rocks and within the deep shade behind palm trees, digging whenever he notices something. Pebbles, shards of gold, even an actual *treasure* are dug up and tossed aside without care.

I don't know what I did. But it feels bad. All the items suddenly stopped working, eyes closed, as if they just … died.

In fact … I am feeling more and more … my eyes can't stay open any longer … look at that soft sand, a perfect bed to lay down for a minute and …

I *feel* like dying.

Everything turns black.

Heartless Pirate

Dying doesn't feel great. Unfortunately, coming back to life later doesn't feel much better.

I feel like I've slept a thousand years and still aren't well-rested. I blink the grains of sand from my eyes to see Sweettooth proudly parade the beach, cheered on by the items, holding a large *heart* over his head.

I instinctively try to move forward, until I realize I'm stuck in this stupid swapping game. All I can do is rotate now, looking at that ship Sweettooth pointed out earlier.

The second counter, which used to be zero, is now one. So it counts hearts. It counts … lives?

Why would a game like this need lives? We're not exactly running around and fighting monsters. Earlier, whenever the Player tried a swap that was wrong, it just *undid* the effect and no life was lost. I think.

You know what I see? A perfect first step to fixing the game.

Sweettooth reaches the ship and places the heart into its hull, which contains five slots with exactly the same size and shape.

"You were digging for that heart, right? How do you know where it is?"

"I don't," he says. "A new one be appearing roughly every five hours. Which is why pirate not be happy when slowed down by some slow-shooting Wildebyte."

"You have to *guess*?"

The other items dare come a little closer. Perhaps they feel the protection of Sweettooth being near.

"They can wash up anywhere," a parrot says. "Whenever the Player makes an attempt at level 1, it costs one heart. And if we run out ..."

A shiver runs through the group. They probably had the same terrible experience I just had. And they have had it *over and over* for as long as this Player had the game.

"That be how I must spend most of my time," Sweettooth says. "Heartsearching. Still interested in joining, aye?"

"That's cruel," I mutter. "How could developers do such a thing? *Why*?"

The answer, as is often the case, appears as a comment. I learned long ago that developers can leave comments or remarks to themselves in the code, which are ignored by the computer. They attach to the closest entity and appear above their head in speech bubbles.

This time, Sweettooth has the comment, even though they desperately try to prevent themselves from revealing it.

We don't know why Sugar Stomp does this, but we're doing it all the same. James, can you implement a life system very quickly before the weekend? Just tie the code into this part here and draw some energy symbols or something.

"I will fix it!" I say. "I'll find a way to turn it off. Watch me."

A few items help me swap *towards* the ship. I don't have to force them anymore. The prospect of *not dying* regularly is probably enticing.

Just before I touch the heart lodged into it, however, Sweettooth pushes me aside, furious.

"Don't be touching that, aye! It is an empty-skulled plan, that is!"

"It's a *great* plan!"

He shakes his head. "All code be connected. You can't be turning off one system at will and expect the game to be still working."

"I can. I believe I know enough to—"

"I say *no!*" They swing their hand at me as if they still have their sword. Lucky for me, they don't. I merely get a slap in my toffee face. "Forget it. Leave the game and don't be returning."

"No! We had a deal!"

"And don't be talking to me again!"

Sweettooth leaves, accompanied by most items in the game. Their movement is like a choreography. By picking the right target for their swaps, at the right time, they all help each other cross through the landscape at speed. Palm trees and rocks are displaced to make it happen, but in such a way that they can easily make the journey *back* at any time.

Some items, however, stay behind. The handful of candy items in this strange mishmash of themes they call—

"This isn't the original," I say at the realization. "This game is blatantly *copying* Sugar Stomp. *Pirate Pound* tries to be like that, but fails."

The candies nod.

"We're … outsiders," a lollipop says. "Not Outsiders, with a capital O, like animals from the real world put into Ludra. Like you."

"But we're outsiders all the same. Most items don't want to swap with us," a gummy bear states sadly. They have a beard made of cotton candy and a candy cane as a walking stick. "It's why I'm by far the oldest item in the game. You shouldn't even get older than 5 plays! But here I am at 100 and counting."

"It's also the reason the Player can hardly win," a chocolate bar says, one with a permanent smile from one end of their bar to the other. "They find a nice match, swipe to swap, and the game just *won't let them*. It pretends it failed."

The chocolate bar displays another comment from the developers.

Who thought it was a good idea to "improve" the original and add items that "hate" each other and won't swap? This is confusing and not-fun. WAS IT YOU JAMES!?

Somewhere in the real world, there's a developer called James being treated pretty much like how I'm treated. I feel for him. On the other hand, he *does* seem to mess up a lot. Maybe switch jobs. I'll tell him if I ever get out.

"Then that's what we need to do," I say. "Get everyone else to swap with you again."

Half their eyes are hesitant; half are hopeful upon hearing my confident plan.

I consider my options, remembering all I've learned from previous games. After an awkward pause, I smile my biggest smile.

"Now this will sound odd, but it will work, believe me."

The lollipop shakes their head at the eagerness of the other candies to try the plan. "We haven't forgotten how you called all of us *mere code* and yourself *better!*"

I should stop talking so loud. Or does it even matter? Could I hear everything being said inside a game if I trained myself to do it? All the sounds are just code too, connected to the rest.

"Look," I try in my softest voice. "I am one of you now, right? Just a helpless little candy—"

"*Helpless? Outrageous!*"

"I misspoke. Just a candy that's treated like an outsider. Let's help each other, right? We are a group, right?"

Despite some hesitation, they agree.

"We are a group, in some way," the chocolate bar says through its smile. "But we can't match. We're different types of candy, nothing will change that."

"All we need to do," I say in my conspiracy voice, "is trick the others into believing you are a different item. Change your clothes, your wrapper. You stay the same on the inside, you follow the same rules and go to Sweethaven if you like, but others will swap with you."

I know just the Native Entity to help us. Someone I met a few games ago and has been the only one that actually treated me well. So I look at the sky and yell, as loud as I can. "Hey Graphics Mover! Come here! We need you!"

As if in response, the Player opens up the game. They were probably notified they had a new heart.

I realize another reason Sweettooth was so *angry* about my plan to remove hearts. It's a great system to keep the player coming back, time and time again. They have to stop playing before they're satisfied … and then get a notification a few hours later inviting them to play again!

Despite that, I still hate the system. Though I can't explain why.

The Camera flies into the game. I expected all the items to be pulled to the level 1 area, like a magnet that attracts them all to the right place. In reality, and this makes sense in hindsight, they are all attracted to the Level Ship.

I hop on too and get a beautiful view of the island from above. The ship is more detailed than it needed to be and it feels like a ride in a theme park. And is that—are those more islands in the distance? The other levels, perhaps?

Once our ride passes over the beach, it *drops* the items into neat stacks, creating the entire playing field.

Just before we can properly start, though, a huge image fills the entire sky. An image showing a different game being played and big letters telling us that game is "the best experience ever" and "addictive" and it will allow us to "live our dream".

Pretty strong words for a game about crossing a road, but okay. It's an advertisement. This game advertises other, better games you could be playing right now. Like reading a book that tells you to read another book halfway through. No wonder we're stuck at level 1!

Initially, once the ad is done, nothing happens. As if this was some random interruption to make the developers more money. Perhaps to make up for all James' mistakes while coding this thing.

Then, Sweettooth dances over the beach again, holding a heart over his head. Waterfalls of sand fall from the heart that was buried not long ago. He pushes it into the ship again, surrounded by cheering items.

I feel better. Everyone feels better. At least we have that one heart of safety before the Great Dying happens. Yes, I'm calling it that. It feels so terrible it needs an ominous name.

Then a new creature walks across the beach. They *walk* instead of swapping. I'm not jealous, you're jealous.

They also wear a suit and are decked out in endless jewelry and expensive-looking items.

"Hi! I'm Ad Brad."

He talks to nobody in particular and emphasizes random words, as if he tries to make "interest" the coolest word on the planet. "Cooooould I interest you in—"

"NO!" all the items yell.

"—the Game Console X1000, the *best thing since sliced bread?*"

He continues speaking through his smile, which is too big for his face. "Or maybe Doll Master XL, a *revolutionary* digital doll-playing game on your phone that will _change your life?"

"You coooooould interest me in some costumes or clothes," I say before he leaves.

He smiles at me—perfect white teeth, and still it shines gold—and jumps on the opportunity.

Then the Player starts playing.

AD BRAD

Talking to Brad is *exhausting*. Doing it while being forced to play the actual game turns it into a wild ride.

The Player tries to swap a candy with a palm tree. It would have made 3 in a row, but the game just forbids it outright. The pirate items simply refuse to swap with the stray candies. I can feel the fun being replaced by frustration, as if I have a direct connection to the Player's emotions.

After searching for a while, they find the only swap they can make that creates a match. Items cry tears of joy as they are let into Sweethaven. I drop down one position in my stack, narrowly dodging the confetti sprays, as if this one swap is the greatest achievement a Player ever reached.

Ad Brad floats in front of me. "Clothes, you say? A costume? What type?"

They start playing another ad, plastered across the tropical sky.

Looking for a wedding dress? Look no further than Gals & Garments, the best you'll ever—

"No! Not clothes in the real world!" Ad-Brad reluctantly closes the ad, muttering something about not getting paid now. "Certainly not wedding dresses."

The Camera is all over the place. The Player's fun and frustration have both made way for utter *confusion*.

Brad turns away. "Be quick about it, my *juiciest toffee I ever saw!* When the player isn't looking, a game is of no interest me."

"In-game disguises," I say quickly. "Something to turn a few items into more pirate-themed items."

The Camera passes by. To my dismay, I notice the interruption cost us a heart. I smile sweetly and feel the Player giving it one more try, using their final heart.

Wait. Whatever happens, win or lose, the heart is gone right? Playing a level *always* costs one life, even if you won. Better hurry then.

"Can you do it or not?"

They smile. "Hi! They call me Ad Brad, and I can do *anything* for the right price. Let's say … 500 Data Doubloons?"

"*Five hundred?*"

After a long search, the Player manages another correct swap. The stack next to me loses 4 items in a column, changing my neighbors entirely. At this pace, I can see the Player falling *asleep* before completing level 1.

Brad impatiently taps my face. "That's the price. But I'm willing to negotiate."

"This isn't for *me!*" I say. "It's for the good of the game. It's the right thing to do."

He laughs, nudging my face like I'm their toddler. "Funny."

"It's not funny. I'm serious."

Ad Brad plays with the collar of his expensive suit. His face is completely neutral, like he's the average of *all* possible eyes, hair colors, noses, dimples, everything. For the first time, he shows a different emotion than a fake smile.

"It doesn't *work* that way, Wildebyte, *most interesting person I ever met.* You have to give away as much as you take. You have to provide *value* to the other person, so they provide *value* back, *value you wouldn't want to miss!*"

This way of talking about living beings makes me nauseous. Like they're some product or resource you discovered deep in the ground. At the same time, he's right. I can't expect him to just give me all I want because I say it's for a good cause.

We enter the Camera frame once more, which forces me to follow the rules and patiently wait for a swap. Brad, however, does a little careless dance.

A special effect appears, counting all the many bonuses and points the Player gets for matching 3 treasure chests. It hides us from view so I can talk again.

"Doesn't the player see you? Why are you so casual about this?"

"Oh, sure, they see me. But everyone has already learned that ads are *everywhere* and they just look past it. *That's life!*"

What can I offer Brad? They already have money. What do they need?

"I can give you *power*. I have ways to cheat Ludra and make miracles happen."

"Not interested," Brad says, turning into salesman voice again. "*Aren't you tired of people saying you need things you don't need? Buy the Headphones 500 Star now, to silence your surroundings!*"

"I can maybe help you travel between games!"

"Not interested."

The Player only has three moves left. They're not going to get enough points, even if they made some miraculous moves. Which is literally impossible, because a quick study of the beach tells me there is literally *no* way to match three of the same items.

Of course. There's no guarantee. The items are just randomly thrown into stacks, which means there's a good chance no matches can ever be made.

I'm sure the developers just have a list of options —all the candies and pirate items—and they randomly pick one for each slot. That simply won't work.

The Player has figured it out. They're closing the level.

"I have something of value to you!" I yell, as our final heart disappears again.

It hurts. Like your heart literally stops, like an illness that never ends, a headache that still hurts even when you sleep. It's a terrible feeling and I never want to feel it again.

As my eyelids droop, I mutter my last statements.

"You want to display more ads? I will fix the game and get it played way more often. I can—"

"No need to explain the details. I don't care. Does it make me more money?"

"Yes! Yes, I think." My eyes close. "I will ... I will ..."

"*Tired all the time? Try the new medicine Ozyxomorpo that will ...*"

Brad's voice fades into darkness. Out of the corner of my eye, Sweettooth slips away, frantically searching for the next heart to wash up on shore.

He's right. Why would he want to travel with me? He's too good for me. He has this fun pirate gimmick, but actually helps the device a lot. Maybe walking between games is a gift from the Memory Police, for his good work.

I need to be better.

Don't say you are better; *be* better.

The last thing I see is the Graphics Mover responding to my call. They enter the game currently dressed as a cute ghost made from twigs and leaves. Then they shapeshift to a larger ghost made of glass.

They talk to Sweettooth and hand him an object, which he quickly stuffs inside a barrel. Then he grabs two small *knives* from his belt, sharpens them, and runs away as if hunting some monster.

I die again, together with all the other items.

An endless nightmare engulfs me, dreaming of dying in Ludra, alone. My code erased due to one mistake too many, never seeing my parents again.

When I wake up, something tells me Sweettooth was in no hurry to find hearts this time. Ah yes. That something is the fact that Ad Brad is gone, the tides have changed to drown half the beach, and an entire *fleet* of pirate ships approaches the island.

They have us surrounded. Sweettooth's fierce eyes betray these are no friends.

Battle for Starter Beach

Sweettooth proudly stands on the bow of his ship, even though it remains stuck in the sand. The attacking fleet consists of 4 ships, all wearing the same flags and logo. Some sort of ... rune? A seemingly ancient symbol that resembles sunglasses placed on their side.

Another pirate, just a black silhouette on the horizon, stands on top of a middle ship.

"Prepare to meet your demise," both pirates yell at each other simultaneously.

My worst fears are confirmed when I notice two more numbers etched into Sweettooth's stuck ship. One is the *current real time* and the other is the *last time played*. The difference between them is several *weeks*. So much time lost.

Yes, that's true, I said it. I fear losing real time more than this oncoming pirate attack.

But why would the game think it so important to track those dates? To rub it in our faces how nobody wants to play this game?

The attacking ships move normally. They cut through the waves, bobbing up and down, and don't need to swap. Although this is probably a fake animation. The waves are drawn in a simple cartoony style and I don't imagine the developers programmed *realistic* water movement.

The pirates on top of them, however, do need to follow the swap rule. The silhouette of their leader swaps with some barrels to move to another part of the ship: the cannons.

"Prepare to fight," Sweettooth yells.

"Who are we fighting? Why?" I ask.

He doesn't answer. "Anything I be saying, you be using against me later."

"You can't expect me to blindly fight for you! I don't even know how to fight without limbs!"

Sweettooth frowns. "Come on, Wildebyte. You be more smart-skulled than that. If you want to impress me, aye."

"Let's just say," the old gummy bear adds, "our terrible lives system wasn't always this way. And we're pretty sure those devils have something to do with it."

"FIRE!"

A cannonball reaches the beach, passing *through* items as if they have no body, to harmlessly fall in the sand and do … nothing?

A second and third cannonball fly into us with similar lack of results. But I am *sure* they went *through* some of those items. What's happening?

Until all cannonballs stop rolling and I notice our attackers have incredible aim: they landed in a perfect 3-in-a-row.

That's when they explode and send all nearby items to …

"Where do you go?" I ask the closest item, a parrot. "If you create a match when the game isn't playing?"

"Not Sweethaven. That's for sure." The parrot looks even more distressed after my question. "Legends say you go to the opposite place."

Three more cannonballs perfectly align to create a match, sending all nearby palm trees to … well, the opposite of Sweethaven I guess. Bitterhell? Sourport? Umamilands?

Anyway, a place I don't want to be.

I try to move out of the way, but only the candy wants to swap with me, and even they are hesitant. The other items create a rapid chain to meet the four identical enemy ships docking at our beach.

Despite knowing where they'll end up, the pirate items start matching on purpose.

Three swords *surround* the ship's mast, like a spear running horizontally through the vertical beam.

And when they complete their lineup, they puff out of existence, taking the entire mast and sail with them.

For the first time, I notice other items of my own type: toffees in a red wrapper. So there *are* way more instances of each item! They eagerly approach me, enough of them to destroy some more parts of enemy ships.

Oh broken buttons. No no. I'm not doing that. I don't even know who I'm fighting or why.

"Coward!" Sweettooth yells. "I be right about you!"

He bravely dashes through enemy pirates pouring in. With precise knife throws, he sends them all to Bitterhell by catching them inside a 3-in-a-row.

The parrot I talked to earlier has already vanished after another salvo of three enemy shots.

I wait until a cannonball flies past me. Then I *swap* with it, lifting myself to a higher position. But because there's nothing below me, I fall down immediately, back to where I started.

I need to time this right.

I wait for the next salvo of shots, wait until they almost form a staircase in the air, then execute a rapid series of swaps. It gets me high enough to land *on top* of a few other items. A safe vantage point to watch the battlefield and—

The ships are indeed identical. That's even more clear from above, with all pirates removed from deck. An idea tickles at the back of my mind, but it feels just out of my grasp.

We seem te be losing, but it's hard to tell. All items are mingled. Swaps happen too fast, matches too explosively, to get a good overview. Half the battle takes place on ships, half on a trampled and soggy beach.

All I see is the leader, a fearsome pirate dressed all in blue. Whereas Sweettooth has one golden tooth, this pirate has more blue teeth than white ones.

The logo from their ships dangles from keychains *everywhere* on their body. Lines radiate from them, like a repeated Wi-Fi symbol or visible radio signal. As if they are constantly in contact with someone else far away.

And the leader isn't fighting at all. They sailed their fourth ship around the battlefield to ransack the beach and caves on the other side.

They found what they were looking for. A treasure that's carefully—but rapidly—loaded onto the ship, as if it were the most precious cargo ever found.

"Sweettooth! They're stealing something from the other side!"

He freezes during a fight with a group of treasure maps. That makes him lose the fight. They match to create a sharp explosion that sends the pirate flying backwards.

Looking back at the battlefield, to the three ships they left behind, my idea finally presents itself.

Three identical ships. Three *identical items*. And they are almost in a row … only the middle ship is lagging behind suspiciously.

"Listen to me!" I yell. "Draw the second ship forward! Have the sails match perfectly with the others!"

Nobody listens to me. A dazed Sweettooth, far below me, scrambles back to his feet. "And why would that be smarrrt, aye?"

"Trust me. Do it now! Before they get away with your—"

"No, I don't trust you."

They continue their useless fight, losing more and more items to Bitterhell. While the enemy has what they wanted and is ready to retreat.

I *force* my stack of items to swap with me and get me onto the beach. Forcing makes me faster, dodging attacks from enemy pirates before I even know they attacked. I just need to stay out of range of other toffees, or I'll accidentally kill myself.

"We're losing precious time!" I yell. Sweettooth ignores me entirely.

I reach the second ship. Somehow it is *easier* to swap with enemy items, as if they don't know who I am yet and haven't learned to protect themselves. I barely have to force anything.

That doesn't change the fact that it takes time. Too much time. Like fighting a headwind for miles and miles, the waves seemingly always pushing *against* me.

The enemy's fourth ship rounds the island. The treasure they stole is well-hidden below deck, replaced by a new item—wait.

A new item with a purple glow. I can't see what it is, but I can feel it is my Lost Memory.

"NO!"

In a flash of understanding, I realize the waves in the sea are also *items*. Just animated blue blocks stacked on top of each other. I swap with them, again, and again, until the second ship is *pushed* by the waves to come forward a little bit more.

Just a little.

Almost in line with the other two ships.

This has to work. If the game has any consistency, this *has* to work.

The second ship slots into place, their bow *perfectly* aligned with the bow of the first and second ship. Ha. Three in a row.

Wait, I'm still—

The ships *explode* and vanish instantly. All items on top of them, such as barrels, furniture, and a few straggler pirates, fall down into the ocean. Otherwise, every hint of the ships are gone.

I know that, because the explosions shot me high into the sky. From there, I have a perfect view of the fourth—and only remaining—ship already fleeing at a safe distance. Holding something dear to Sweettooth, and something even more dear to me.

"CURSE YOU, BLUETOOTH!" Sweettooth yells into the empty ocean.

With a frustrated sigh, I prepare for the long fall back to the sand.

No Choice

The other candy items were the first to visit me. After some required questions such as "are you alright?" and "you know you're not supposed to eat sand?", they congratulated me and told me I was amazing.

Most of all, though, they wanted to know one thing.

"Is the mission still on?" the elderly gummy bear asks in a whisper. "The one about tricking the others into swapping with us?"

He looks hopeful. Eager. His chance to reach Sweethaven after more than a hundred plays is in my hands—or, well, toffee wrappers.

I look to the side and my heart jumps with joy. The Graphics Mover came back and smiles at me.

"I'm sorry about your Lost Memory, darling." They change into a ghost plush toy. "I found it on my way into the game, and gave it to Sweettooth for safekeeping until you woke up. Didn't know an entire battle would break out!"

"It's … it's fine," I say, removing the last grains of sand from my tongue. "I was hoping you could help."

They raise an eyebrow, drawn like a rough pencil sketch. "With your … mission?"

"It's for the good of the game."

Yeah, because that argument worked so well on Ad Brad. I'm assuming he didn't care about my offers and just left with a shrug. Only money matters to him. Pff, I don't even *want* to work with that sneaky snaky guy, thank you very much.

Surprisingly, the Graphics Mover shrugs and smiles affirmingly. "Well then, darling, what do I do?"

I smile as I explain the plan. They all listen to me and want to work with me. Are these my people? Have I found a place I belong? It feels like it.

As we wait for the Player to play again, the candies help me swap towards Sweettooth. But now, of course, they don't look like candy anymore. The Graphics Mover manipulated their appearance so they now wear the *model*, from memory, of palm trees or treasure chests. If you look closely, you can see it doesn't match their code or content at all—so let's hope nobody looks closely.

"We be dealing them a great blow, aye? Aye?" I say to Sweettooth in their scruffy accent, almost snuggling up to them.

They swat me to the side. "Don't be imitating me, demon."

"Oh come on. I did well," I tease him and pitch my voice higher. "I won't tolerate this attitude when we start Gamewalking together, young man!"

"Arrr! Stop saying that word! Stop rubbing it in!" he bellows.

This feels strange. To get so mad about nothing. I remember Ad Brad's words and try one last time.

"I did something for you! The least you can do is give me something back."

"You be empty-skulled about how friendship works," he grumbles. I have to let him go, as he starts another search for new hearts on another part of the island.

He's probably just stressed. Overworked. Pirate burnout? Something like that.

Especially because Bluetooth seemed like a recurring problem. An enemy that came to fight many times before.

Apparently, he ruined their Lives System. I like to see that in a positive way: it means you can mess with the game's systems without breaking it entirely. It means we can go back to a better system, the one from before.

The candy items are eager to help me. When I ask about the location of their Level Ship, they draw a whole treasure map to point me to the exact location. To get there, I still need to swap against the will of a few parrots and rocks, but that's all for the good of the game.

Because once I reach that ship, I can touch it and look into its code.

"I am Barno," the old gummy bear says. He insisted on coming along and helping. "They say a lot of things about you, Wildebyte."

"I'm sure they do."

I touch the hull until I get the best view at the code inside. For the most part, it's still just spheres showing 0s and 1s, running around on tracks. But the last game taught me a bit more about numbers and code, allowing me to recognize meaningful *words* here and there.

Barno is amazed by the sight. Lesson learned: normally, other creatures in this world *can't* see inside code.

"Maybe we got a bit carried away. Maybe we believed them rumors too easily. You are a sweetie, on the inside ... and outside at the moment." He places two soft arms on my head. "We'd love for you to be a part of our group."

His words distract me from my task. I'm tempted to just turn around and hug the Barno bear, but I have more important tasks now.

"Thanks," I quickly say.

I point at some of the tracks that are now visible around the ship. "This game has more than enough duplicates of each item. Levels should be much easier, matches more frequent. But it doesn't happen. Why?"

Barno shrugs. "We were hoping you—"

"That was a rhetorical question. I do that when I'm talking through things."

"Okay. Whatever floats your boat."

"The developers *programmed* it that way."

I tap the flying ship to reveal a comment.

The game shouldn't be too easy!!! James, here's a todo: write a check for how many matches there are, and limit it to at most 1 or 2. Purposely add a random and different item every time to ensure nothing matches.

"In trying to make it harder, they removed all … choice. And now we've seen how little is left of a game when you don't actually have a choice!"

Barno nods. He strokes his cotton candy beard, as if about to say something wise and philosophical. "I see. The Player is just executing the one thing the game allows them to do, which isn't fun, right?"

"So …"

Well, here goes nothing.

I close my eyes and send energy into the ship, modifying that part of the code. And hopefully *only* that part. Instead of forcing only 1 possible match each time, I just remove the restriction. Let them pick randomly from a small set of items. Then you actually have a large *chance* of getting possible matches, right?

In the end, I merely *ripped* a chunk of code out of the Level Ship. Less control about the random level generation. And just in time, because the vehicle suddenly powers on and aims to meet the Camera flying into the game.

Let's see my changes in action.

I can feel the Player's emotions. They are almost … reluctant? As if they already gave up on the game before even trying level 1 again. I can't blame them. Barno's face also mirrors the Player's current emotions.

"Let's prove them wrong," I say.

As we get sucked into the Level Ship, Barno also changes appearance to a parrot, and I become some sort of scary octopus. A kraken, that's how the Graphics Mover called. Well, they called it a *kraken darling*, but it doesn't look so sweet.

One by one, the ship drops the items into the familiar stacks. This time, however, only 6 different items appear. No candy. Only half the pirate items.

And my changes prove correct when the ship drops *three parrots in a row* by accident, into the same stack! Which the game instantly recognizes. They disappear and the gaps are refilled.

The Camera zooms in. It watches more closely, the Player suddenly at the edge of their seat and interested.

They start swapping left and right.

Confetti sprays, loud sound effects, points upon points trip and fall into a new highscore. And that's only after a few moves.

The Player creates a new match: *4-in-a-row*. Four parrots in a straight line. Of course you can do that! They just never had the chance before!

The Player's fun increases alongside the joy from the items and their highscore. Because 4-in-a-row obviously yields way more points than a boring 3-in-a-row. Item after item chants and sings as they are allowed into their precious Sweethaven, whatever or wherever that may be.

Then the Player hovers around a disguised candy. I think the chocolate bar is inside, but I'm not sure—all I see now is a sword.

They use it to swap with a real sword.

I close my eyes, already imagining that error sound and my plan failing.

But the swap succeeds!

The fake sword is now on the other side; three real swords match and enter Sweethaven in a rain of sparkles.

Now the Player's thumb moves to Barno, disguised as a parrot. Yes! It's working! And—

Wait, the Player will create two matches at once, without knowing it. Because in the next column, where Barno will end up, two more gummy bears are waiting. If they swap Barno with a real parrot, they'll match both 3 parrots and 3 gummy bears.

The Player does it. Heaps and heaps of points shower onto the beach, eagerly collected by Sweettooth's ship that's keeping score with a simple integer bolted to its hull.

They've reached the threshold. They did it! They passed Level 1. And with a handful of moves left!

The other items are shocked by this reveal. A swap between a candy and non-candy? And the game gives you loads of *points* for it?

The shock and disgust turns into a wave of eagerness. They all want to be the next one to do it.

And then the sad realization hits me. Barno is gone. They've fulfilled their dream of reaching Sweethaven, which seems to imply they never return.

This will happen to every candy, now more quickly than ever.

It will happen to me if I don't—

"Stop! Don't swap that!"

Two red toffees are coming dangerously close. The Player continues the swap, removing a few palm trees and dropping the other toffees almost in line with me.

One more swap and I'm gone. The Player won't do it, right? To their eyes I look like a kraken!

A very juicy kraken, apparently, because they try to use me for something anyway.

I don't belong here. I can't be part of these items, of this group, because my goals are entirely different. I don't want to die! I don't want to go to Sweethaven!

"Stop!"

I remove my disguise. The fake kraken returns to being a toffee. It causes just enough hesitation in the Player's twitchy fingers to delay the swap.

And with my new understanding of the game, and sheer willpower, I turn myself into a *different item*.

Not a candy. One of the pirate items that's not on the current playing field.

The Player beats level 1 for the first time. It triggers a huge chain of huge consequences, and I am still alive to see it.

SHARP SHOTS

The Player immediately wants to try level 2, which they just unlocked, which takes us to the *other* side of the island. The side where Bluetooth stole a precious treasure from Sweettooth. I don't see how more levels could fit on this tiny island, but maybe the game surprises me.

I study my new shape. Metal, heavy, a long neck— I'm a pirate pistol. A flintlock, it says. The only one of its kind, as far as I can tell. Maybe it was only supposed to unlock at, like, level 10. I am able to stand upright with my face at the end of the barrel, and the grip as single leg. Not great, but it's improvement.

The fun from the Player courses through my veins. They swap at will in this second level, because almost anything creates a match. In fact, they play several rounds before they even have to think before doing a swap.

For the first time, they hesitate for more than a hundred frames.

This unlocks a new part of the code: hints. Helpful white circles pop up to show the Player which items are a possible swap. They eagerly take the hint and continue.

After only three attempts, they beat level 2. They desperately want to continue playing, but they ran out of lives. I sense frustration and curiosity from the Player in equal measure.

A button pops up. A temporary one, which means we will all *die* again in ten seconds if not pressed. It offers to view another advertisement in return for a life.

The Player decides to do it.

Are you tired of your kids forgetting their backpack when going to school? No more! With the Burden Backpack XL, it will be permanently glued to their back! As an added bonus, this makes it impossible to sleep, so they also won't oversleep and arrive too late! Buy it now for the low low price of 100 dollars.

Ad Brad walks our beaches again. As the player searches for level 3, he tries to sell stuff to anyone nearby.

"Coooooould I interest you in—"

"NO." A grumpy parrot squeaks.

"Hey! Let me finish! I'm exercising my *free speech* here, *the most important thing in the world!*"

"I'm exercising my wings," they say as they fly away through a series of swaps with *clouds.*

This continues until Ad Brad reaches me. Somehow, he can still instantly tell I'm the Wildebyte, despite my new model.

"Ah. You again. I see you found someone else to give you clothes."

"Yes. Someone who didn't ask money."

Brad frowns. "Then they are stupid and will soon be broke. *And everybody looooves having money, so get your lottery ticket now and—*"

I grin. Which probably looks quite scary when combined with a pistol. "They will never be broke. I think they are *much* smarter than you, Brad, and you will soon be out of business."

His face flushes red. "Impossible! Ads run the world! Ad is *literally* in my name!"

He's so angry he forgets to sell something for once. He stays with me, even after the opportunity to make money in this game has already passed.

"Who are they? Tell me. Tell me and I'll show you they are charlatans, fake tricksters, *and we build our community on trust and transparency!*"

My grin deepens. I *have* found something else he *values*, besides money. His status and his pride.

"I will tell you." I continue the lie, talking loudly so all pirate items around me can hear. "If you just give the player infinite hearts without having to watch your ads."

He scowls. Then he waggles his finger at me. "No no, you're lying. This can't be true. You're manipulating me! So it is true what they say about you, dark demon."

Still red-faced and red-bodied, he quickly leaves the game.

Where is that level 3? The Player also gives up trying to find or unlock it. They leave the game alone, their initial fun mostly replaced by frustration again. It's a miracle they keep coming back at all, at this point.

A treasure chest swaps places to stand next to me. Or sit next to me. Or however you call it.

"We haven't seen you before," he says.

"Wow! You're a new item. You're the *original*," a sword on the other side proclaims.

Suddenly, they are all very interested in me. What do they mean with "original"?

Wait a minute, I know the answer myself. In a previous game, all characters only existed once in the code. They were just *duplicated* to visually appear as an entire town of characters.

This game probably does the same. Each item is just one tiny model and piece of code, but they ask the computer to *display* it in many different places. So I'm the original flintlock pistol and soon there will be copies of me inside levels.

"Swap with me?" the treasure chest offers. "Maybe it gives us some special abilities or something!"

"No! No! Swap with me!" a palm tree tries.

Well, can't do any harm, right? I let it happen, first swapping with the chest, then the palm tree, then four other items.

Nothing special happens. It's a little disappointing, but at least I've shown them that I can be trusted. They stop moving away and I don't have to force them to swap anymore.

I didn't belong with the candy. Maybe I belong here?

"So what's your deal? Any fun activities? Powers?" I ask.

They look at each other. "Well, no. Didn't somebody already tell you? We want to get a perfect match in-game so we can all go to Sweethaven!"

I sigh. "So you're exactly the same like the candy? Just looking different?"

"We are *so* not the same!" a parrot starts, but she is shut up by the others.

"Maybe it was wrong of us to cast them aside," the chest speaks, with a low and deep voice. "Just as it was wrong to cast you aside, Wildebyte. We've all seen you try and help the game numerous times now."

"Such acts," the parrot now says, "are probably enough to forget the *insults* you spoke."

I want to ask "what insults?" but that would probably be another insult. You just can't win when playing *that* game.

But now I have to cast them aside.

"I don't belong here. You know I don't. So thanks for the kind words and swapping with me, but I really *don't* want to end up in Sweethaven. It seems a stupid goal to me."

Ugh, that came out wrong.

They look as if I've insulted them, their parents, their pets, and their entire family. Disappointment, anger, betrayal, it all radiates from them like the squiggly lines that radiated from Bluetooth. The same squiggly lines that come from a cave on this other side of the island, as if it's constantly calling someone.

The entire life of these items is centered around Sweethaven and matching, and I couldn't be more different.

"You are right," the parrot says in a sharp tone, "we are *so* not a match!"

Sweettooth barges into the conversation, swapping away some of the angriest items. "Yarr, yarr, you can get angry at Wildebyte later. There be plenty of opportunities, I be sure. Now I need your help."

"My help too?" I ask as the others walk away.

"NO!" is the unanimous response.

"Stay where you be doing no harm," Sweettooth says. "Search for new Lives that wash ashore."

I almost do it. So eager to please the pirate, apparently. But what for? It's like everyone told themselves they *must* be angry at me and it's forbidden to even show a single bit of kindness.

Wait. Maybe it is really forbidden? The Memory Police forced everyone in this game to hate me? Yes, I suspect foul play from the Native Entities.

"Graphics Mover! Come!" I yell into the sky. We *really* need a better way of communicating.

But maybe this is for the best. A large dose of sadness crept into my cry and made them come rather quickly. They currently look like a flabby ghost made of paper and cardboard.

"You sounded truly distressed, darling. But now I see you are in no danger."

"Some of the biggest danger," I say with eyes cast down, "can't be seen."

They frown and come sit beside me on the beach, watching the waves roll in as the sun sets. It's beautiful here. I should be happy. I even understand the swapping now, because most items don't have legs for walking or arms for swinging.

"This isn't like you, darling. Where's that *action* and *adventure*? Those confident plans? Ruining a game but fixing it at the same time? Head held high?"

"Stomped into a sandy beach by characters who all hate me," I mutter.

They smile at me and warmth fills my heart. "I don't hate you, darling. Remember that the Native Entities *voted* and more than half wanted to keep you around because you could do real *good* for Ludra."

"Yeah. But that's just because I had *value* to you, like Ad Brad says. You just wanted to keep me for my skills in changing code, not … not for *me*!"

The Graphics Mover changes into a fluffy unicorn, though their eyes never really change from their ghostlike appearance. "So prove them wrong, darling. Whining about it won't help the situation."

"Ouch."

They giggle and nudge me. "Sorry, darling. Didn't mean to take such a … sharp shot at you. But you needed to hear that."

How didn't I see this before? There already *are* entities that can cross between games.

The Native Entities.

Perhaps … I belong there.

"Dear Graphics Mover, I have a weird question."

THE MISSING PIECE

I never get to ask my question, because the Graphics Mover also took the Memory Police with them.

"We ask the questions, troublemaker!" Their pincers push me and the mover apart. As if they're my dad trying to prevent me from getting too intimate with someone of the opposite gender.

"It seems I was right," their raw voice says. "I don't know what you did, Wildebyte. But ever since you landed here, no other game has reported break-ins or trouble anymore!"

"*Break-ins?*"

"Yeah. Some pirate breaking in and walking through their game like they own it. Sometimes a cookie was also involved. Money stolen, mechanics changed, exits left open. Caused some *real* issues in that zoo game when the lions ... anyway, how did you do it?"

"Honestly," I say, "I did nothing. I improved the game in a minor way. And then we got attacked by a fearsome Pirate."

"You never do nothing Wilde—wait, a fearsome pirate?"

"Yeah. Bluetooth. Stole my Lost Memory and some treasure from Sweettooth. It's basically our big enemy in this game."

"Why does a match-three game need an *enemy*?" The Police shakes their head. "Troublemakers, all of them."

They grab the Graphics Mover. "Come with me. We have lots of work to do! No chitchatting with our peasants!"

She looks apologetically and mumbles sorry, as the imposing Police drags her away like a ragdoll.

Okay. Maybe I can't be friends with *all* Native Entities. I have only really met a handful of them.

I'm left on my own. Without anybody to swap with, I literally can't move around. Sure, I can swap with the blocks of water or the blocks of sand, but that just brings me underwater or underground.

Could I reach Bluetooth all on my own? Keep swapping with water until I reach their ship and steal back the Lost Memory? A quick glance at the ocean makes me doubt that plan. It would take hours to reach the next island, shrouded in mist. And something tells me that this game has more than two islands.

But I *need* my Lost Memory as much as I *need* someone with whom to Gamewalk.

Haven't I already done enough for this game? Why do I need to provide *value* to others before they treat me like a friend?

I … I have every right to move around this island!

As soon as some items come close to me, I use them to swap in the general direction of Sweettooth's departure. I need to follow footprints—or rather *swapprints*—and vague noises for a while before I close in on their location.

The sun has set. A few bright torches fighting the darkness give away Sweettooth's location.

I arrive at the other side of the island, hidden behind some palm trees and—oh dang it, those are living palm trees, I can't hide.

Before I get a chance to settle down, they swap around to harshly cast me into the middle of the clearing.

The items have gathered here like it's a sacred ceremony. Two treasure chests are placed in front of a large rock. The rock itself doesn't look natural—too round and too smooth. Probably a door leading to the cave behind it.

A few torches burn to the sides, doing almost nothing to expel the darkness after sunset. Sweettooth looks at me disapprovingly. To my surprise, however, they don't force me away.

The two chests look identical to what was stolen from Sweettooth. They are placed to the left and right with a clear gap in the middle for one more chest like that.

"Bluetooth stole the third one," Sweettooth says. "Which be a problem, aye, because we need to match three in a row to open this cave door."

"And there aren't any more?" I ask.

"No there be not." Sweettooth caresses the other treasures. "They stole the most important one."

"How can one be more important when you need to match three identical items?"

"Later," he says dismissively. "Arr! It be supposed to be this big reveal, with a nice animation and everything! The true start of the game, after the tutorial. But Bluetooth be ruining it. Now we need to manually open this door to get the treasure map behind it. "

"Which will ..."

Sweettooth looks more menacing when standing next to a blazing torch. It contradicts his bright smile and flickering eyes at the following words: "It will unlock all the next levels, finally letting the Player progress to level 3 and beyond!"

"They haven't returned in almost a day!" one of the item cries out. "They never stay away this long!"

"This is how it always goes," another mutters. "They will uninstall the game if we don't get that treasure map soon! They assume the game is completely broken."

"Oh," another high cry, "we are *so* getting uninstalled!"

"Please," I plead, "let me help. I can help."

For the first time, Sweettooth is at a loss for words. He is slowly losing control of the situation and has no solution to the missing treasure. His anger about the theft won't magically bring it back.

My mind starts racing.

"Okay, so the game accepts any match with 3 or more items, right?" I say.

"As far as we can tell. Never saw one with 5 yet, though. Must give a *bazillion* points!"

"That means there must be some part in the code that has this number." I want to pace around as I think, but I don't want to do anything to scare the items again. So I become an awkward statue between the treasures. "Some part of the code checks how *long* a match is—how many identical items are in a row—but only accepts it if it's 3 or higher."

"So," I say with a smile, "if we can lower that number to 2, we can get in. Because we have 2 treasures."

"Assuming Bluetooth don't be attacking again soon," he says.

"Yes, yes." My hand already moves to the treasure to look at the code inside. A first starting point. But I hold myself back and ask: "Do I have permission to touch the treasures?"

Sweettooth responds to my new behavior with a slight grin and a wink. "Aye."

The objects don't give me any answers, though. Just plain old chests. But they must be connected to the matching code somehow. Because that code is inside *everything.* Like a tiny string that connects them to … the Codeheart? That's the beating heart that runs the essential code for each game.

"I ask permission to look at the Codeheart. Where is it?"

"Now that be a big ask, it be."

"Oh, come on. Killing the Codeheart would instantly shut down the game, killing me too. I'm not that empty-skulled, as you say, thank you very—" I quickly undo my aggressive tone. "I mean, please Sweetooth? Pretty please?"

They nod again, approving of this change. Their face softens and they speak more like a teacher trying to help someone understand.

"It be a big ask because the Codeheart be pretty hard to reach."

An alarm goes off. Another attack? No, even with the weak lighting, I see a clear ocean without ships on the horizon.

Also, no alarm went off to warn us of the last attack. That should worry me more than it does.

"What is it?" I demand of the crazed items swapping at random.

The clouds and stars in the sky are replaced with *erasers*. Like an army of angry mosquitoes ready to attack and pounce on this helpless game world. A swarm of rectangle-shaped insects ready to devour the island.

"Uninstall! Uninstall!"

"The Player is about to uninstall!"

Two buttons appear in the sky, one a beautiful safe painting that says "Cancel", the other a dreadful red button that says "Uninstall".

"Do something interesting!" My panicked yell echoes across the entire island. "Get the Player's attention!"

"What does that *mean*!?"

"I don't know! Dance! Invent new mechanics! Show some ridiculous ad!"

I notice the squiggly lines around the closed cave again. The same radio waves I saw around Bluetooth, like a cartoon effect to signal the cave is shaking or rumbling. But the cave isn't moving at all. Is this game connected to the internet? Is it talking to something else?

The Player's frustration with the game is tangible. They are so done with this mess.

Their finger reaches for the Uninstall button.

I gamble. I touch the cave and try to activate whatever causes the squiggly lines.

The Player presses Uninstall.

Just before they did, however, a different window popped up. Which means they now accidentally pressed a completely different button that did something they didn't want. Sorry, Player, but not sorry.

ONE GRAY BLOB

The uninstall is averted, but the Player isn't happy. They accidentally sent all the extra Lives they had to a friend of them, as a gift. Now we're down to one life again. Oh, they also accidentally sent all powerups—called Pirate Legends—they collected.

Their friend responds quickly to the gift.

> **JumpyFlamingo10**: Wow thanks! But you should keep playing, really.

> **PresidentNotMyDad:** This game is stupid :(Finally got past level 2, then level 3 just never unlocks. It's broken. Stupid.

I sigh at the choice of username by our Player. The President really has to give his kids some media training or something. All I know is that I'm in the President's old phone, but I don't know any other details about our Player. I hope these conversations might change that.

> **JumpyFlamingo10**: I know it's hard. But it gets more and more fun as you go! I'm

already at level 10.

PresidentNotMyDad: HarD?!? The game is way too easy now!

JumpyFlamingo10: Huh?

PresidentNotMyDad: And don't remind me you're way ahead of me. Ugh :((

JumpyFlamingo10: Seriously, how can you call this game easy?

PresidentNotMyDad: Everything matches now! Some update or something. It doesn't matter what I do, it all leads to basically the same thing. These developers SUCK! They should KILL THEMSELVES for making such a TERRIBLE GAME :(((

JumpyFlaming10: Wow :o Calm down! Jeez.

I freeze upon reading the messages, which appear as speech bubbles above the cave. Every new message bounces off of the previous one, as if the game tries to swap the speech bubbles too.

I hadn't considered that. First the game had basically no choice. Then I allowed *everything* to match, almost *everything* be a valid swap, and thought I did great.

But this just means the player doesn't even *have* to make a choice anymore. Anything they do works. Anything they do has the same effect.

Having a hundred meaningless choices is just the same as having none at all. The game becomes one gray blob of the same choice over and over.

"You be a great influence, you arrr," Sweettooth says sarcastically. He spits past me.

> **JumpyFlamingo10**: If you hate it so much, why do you come back at all?

> **PresidentNotMyDad**: Can't break my streak. Skipping a day means losing my x4 bonus on Pirate Legend rewards on Sundays. THIS GAME SUCKS ASS.

> **JumpyFlamingo10**: Yeah. Sure. It's not because I'm already at level 10 and you're stuck at level 2, right? CATCH UP.

The chat closes. Some more profile pictures float over the cave. They have many friends playing the game, and all are ahead of them.

Yeah, alright, I'll admit. That would've motivated me to play the game every day as well. But I would never let my friends beat me, I'm too good a gamer for that, thank you very much.

I'm starting to doubt whether this game should even be given to kids to play. Those are some strong words by what I assume is a young son or daughter of the president. And it's not some fake sentiment. I feel the Player really means what they say. So angry. Yet so addicted to the game.

At least they recognized it themselves, as they were prepared to uninstall. Unfortunately, that cannot happen.

"We need to—"

"We not be doing anything together," Sweettooth and the items say in unison. "Even the Player, with the odd-pistoled username, be arrgreed you're a bad influence!"

They leave me in the dust once more. Alone. Always alone.

Maybe total freedom isn't all that. Maybe it was good to steer the Player into a few fun choices. Maybe sometimes you have to admit the game or the rules know better than you.

I try the one thing I haven't tried before. Stop making my own decisions and doing my own thing all the time.

It takes a while before items pass me by again. I ask them to relay a message to Sweettooth. A crucial message, an urgent one, not to be remembered incorrectly.

Not long after, Sweettooth himself appears next to me.

"You be sure? *You pledge to follow all my commands without hesitation? And never be doing your own* empty-skulled business, aye?"

I swallow. The game converts it into an animation that reloads my pistol, despite having no bullets in the first place.

"Yes. I do whatever you say."

"How can I be sure you be keeping a promise?" He holds another Life under his armpit, as if he carries a nice wooden stick he found in the jungle instead of the most precious resource in this game.

"If I make so much as *one* decision myself, kick me out of the game or have the Memory Police arrest me. You know they *want* to have a reason to do it."

He grunts. "Then we have an arrrgreement."

Sweettooth swaps away, leaving me behind.

"Eh? Sweettooth?" I stay in the sand. I just said I wouldn't make any decisions myself! And I'm sticking to that!

"Aye, right. Follow me closely. We be visiting the Codeheart and changing the game rules."

A series of swaps leads us deeper into the island, closer to the jungle at its center. An obvious place for a Codeheart. Even before reaching it, we have to perform some odd swaps to dodge around thick vines and unswappable fallen branches.

Sweettooth does a *diagonal* swap, both to the side and up at the same time.

"Wow," I say. "You gotta teach me that."

"You be already having the skill, aye," he says. "Only the Player be forbidden from doing it."

My mind has started to understand this world. How it's entirely made of blocks put into a sort of grid. Rows horizontally, laid over the beach like a blanket, and columns vertically, reaching into the sky. Just like the x-axis and y-axis of the previous game!

Finding an item to your right, means finding the item at your X position plus 1.

Finding an item above you, means finding the item at your Y position plus 1.

So swapping diagonally ... means swapping with the item at $X + 1$ and $Y + 1$.

As this clicks in my head, I am able to do it and follow Sweettooth with ease.

Nearing the center of the island, the jungle grows too thick and creates an impenetrable wall. The green web of vines, trees and inanimate insects has no gap at all.

"I assume the Codeheart is behind ... *that?*"

I look up. The wall goes higher than any stack in the levels so far. So no use climbing over it.

"How did you reach it before? You said it was hard, not impossible."

Sweettooth is hesitant to reveal the answer. He waits until the other items are out of earshot.

"Luck," he whispers in his rough voice. "I returned from another game and be falling into it, out of the sky, aye. I not be the skilled pirate you think I be, Wildebyte."

"Ugh, and you're *humble* too," I mutter softly. "How can I ever live up to that?"

Sweettooth doesn't seem to hear. Their eyes scan the green wall wrapped around the island's center for any opening.

I realize something else. Swapping just means having two items switch places. One item picks where it wants to be, such as its X position plus 1, then moves there. It tells the other item where it came from, so it can move there, and we're done.

But if we can pick our destination ourselves ... what's stopping us from picking X + 2 or Y + 2? Swapping with something not directly next to us? Not our neighbor, but something *just* a little further away?

"Now, Wildebyte," Sweettooth says without looking. "You be careful and be listening to my instructions. Because the Codeheart is protected by—"

I close my eyes, reach for the position *behind* the green wall, and find something there. I swap with it.

When I open my eyes, I am *inside* the green shield. The Codeheart, a glimmering purple heart that's larger than me, beats against my side. I'm afraid it accidentally triggers my pistol, so I turn away. Their veins send endless signals into the game, like rivers coursing through the island to eventually reach the ocean.

This reveals that "shield" was the right word. Because the other items near the Codeheart are *other pirates* programmed to protect it at all costs.

And I just swapped one of them out into the real island, right next to Sweettooth.

His curses reach my ears as a battle ensues.

Match Thy Neighbor

I instantly swap back to the other side, through the green shield. Where's Sweettooth?

Oh. Now he curses me from the other side. I accidentally swapped with *him*.

I move a little further and swap through the protection again. I narrowly dodge a sword slice from a pirate as I glide past Sweettooth using his hat as a shield.

"You promised to make no more decisions!" he yells. "Follow my commands only!"

"I know! I know!" I duck as Sweettooth does some pirouette move, slapping three pirates into the vines with his hat. "I'm sorry! This is new to me! I'll listen now!"

"Reinforcements!" he yells.

I close my eyes to properly count the positions on the other side of the shield. By swapping myself in and out, I am able to move more and more items in there with Sweettooth.

But at the cost of moving more and more pirates *out* of it.

"Why do you fight us?" I say. "We're on the same team!"

The pirate before me gives no answer. Can they not speak? They are much smaller than Sweettooth. Less strong and less equipped, as if they were the first draft and Sweettooth the final version.

"Come back!" yells Sweettooth.

I follow his command and instantly return to him. He *uses* me for a last-minute swap, forcing *me* to receive the blow from a pirate's fist. This does allow him to spin around and push the pirate out of position, forming a match with two other pirates.

"Three pirates in a row!" I yell triumphantly.

But ... they don't disappear. Oh yes, they do, but *very slowly*.

This allows me to see the process: one starts to glow, then infects the one next to them, which infects the one next to them. Only once the infection cannot spread to another neighbor—and all matching items are glowing—do all infected items disappear. I call it an infection, because that's what it looks like to me. But the code probably just sets some value shouldRemove to true on the pirates.

The Codeheart looks enticing, like a diamond any reasonable pirate would want to collect. But in this chaos it struggles to keep up. That's why the matching slows down. That's why everything seems to happen in slow-motion.

"Duck!"

I obey without hesitation. A frame later, my pistol body feels the wind from a swinging sword just above the barrel.

Oh broken buttons. Sweettooth has that same glow as well, starting a match. There is no other pirate like him, though, so he doesn't infect anyone else and it breaks down. Pfew.

A few parrots next to me aren't that lucky. The middle one starts to glow, which infects the one on the right and the one on the left, quickly creating a 3-in-a-row.

Now that I can see the effect, I notice the glow can start anywhere. One by one, each item is considered by the Codeheart, trying to infect identical neighbors. If they find one, they continue to infect neighbors of the same type. If they find none, they stop.

And if the infection ever reaches 3 items or more, it's a match.

And I'm here to change that number to a 2.

But not without Sweettooth's permission. I've learned from my mistakes.

It takes ages for him to notice and point at the Codeheart.

"Fix it, Wildebyte," him and the other items yell. I asked for this, I guess. It's a command, not a question. Ugh, now I know how the other items felt when I forced them to swap.

I touch the Codeheart to look at its code. I'm getting better at it: recognizing some words or logical connections, instead of just clouds of white 0s and black 1s. Now I'm looking for the code that "infects".

Is that what the developers called it? They probably just went with *matching* or maybe *grouping*.

Match your neighbor. Check all neighbors to find a match. Spread the matchiness. Three-in-a-rowify. Infectinize. Something like that?

As I search, Sweettooth sometimes tells me to "swap to the left" or "duck" or "sing a powerful warrior song" and I obey without—a warrior song?

Sweettooth laughs at me as I already started singing nonsense lyrics.

"Not funny!"

"Oh I be thinking it *very* funny, aye."

There it is. An integer—a thick green number 3—is pushed into the back of the Codeheart. A track leads from the integer to the word `matchNeighborsOfItem`.

I point at it, yelling for Sweettooth's attention. They nod.

I change the integer to a 2. Now only two items need to be neighbors to get a match.

This change instantly causes a large number of pirates and items to vanish. They stood side by side, thinking they'd be safe, and weren't prepared.

"Sorry," Sweettooth and I whisper simultaneously.

"Get us out! Aye!"

I rapidly swap items to safety through the green shield. More and more, I am able to perfectly swap them with a position I can't even see. At the same time, I must be careful to bring the angry pirates *back* to the Codeheart area.

Because of that, we all missed the Player coming back. They had another conversation with a friend in the "Social Hub" of this game.

> **PresidentNotMyDad**: This is STUPID! It's so easy to match now that the game plays itself and I don't do anything!

> **JumpyFlamingo10**: You sure you're playing the same game as me???

The cloud fills with *erasers* again: wasps even hungrier than the last time. The sky has another message asking the Player if they want to Uninstall.

No hesitation. No savior.

They press the button to *Uninstall Pirate Pound*.

I can't do anything about it this time.

The glitches and distortions in the environment are the first sign that the uninstall is really happening. Rocks flicker in and out of existence, palm trees collapse into pixelated chaos, and the erasers rain down on us. My old toffee comrades are the first to be completely removed from the game. The pirates we're fighting glitch in and out of visibility, turning it into a fight with ghosts half the time.

Getting uninstalled is almost as bad as dying in this game because the Lives ran out. If I wasn't *in* here, I wouldn't want to even save this game. But I'll have to make do with what I have.

Palm trees suddenly lack either branch or leaves. Erasers chase the items around, like nipping predators.

And the items make themselves easy prey. They run into each other, or decline any swaps, or huddle in a corner so a single eraser can get them *all* at the same time.

I don't know what to do. This is really happening. I failed, I failed, I failed.

More and more of the island just turns into nothingness. The ocean drains like a sink and the remaining holes vortexes that suck in anything that still moves. To my eyes, the erasers grow angry eyes and a snarling mouth with sharp teeth.

I freeze for the longest time. Unable to form a word, unable to form a thought, as I stare death in its unforgiving eyes.

"Stacks of ten!" Sweettooth yells, standing on top of the highest rock. He looks bigger than before. "Rows of twenty. To my ship."

I immediately copy his commands. The items start to form orderly rows, creating swapping chains that lead most of them to the ship, which is safe for now.

We are getting ahead of the erasers.

"Wildebyte, run to that palm tree!"

Don't think. Do. I race to that specific spot, though I don't see the significance. I wait there, still frozen. Sweettooth is the only one with a good picture of the entire situation, steering his loyal items to where they need to go.

Only now do I notice the three erasers tailing me. They *really* want to erase me. I feel honored, thank you very much. And also terrified. My pistol keeps reloading and trying to shoot bullets it doesn't have.

They must fly in a weird curve to reach me behind the palm tree. This forces them to make three in a row—and the game obliges in making them disappear.

The hard sand of the beach turns into quicksand. The entire level 1 area has been erased. Next to me, the final lollipop candies puff away. And all that time, the alarm blares and adds a nasty peep into my hearing.

"There are too many!" I yell at Sweettooth.

"That be the words of an empty-hearted!" he yells back, still king of the hill, master of the operation. At his command, a large part of the game has safely reached his ship. Is it invulnerable? Surely not. Uninstall means uninstall.

He doesn't command me to visit the ship.

He's leaving me behind.

He isn't, right? Right?

I should ... I have to ...

But his commands made sense until now. He saved me just now.

"What do I do?" I yell at Sweettooth. He's too preoccupied to answer.

So I stay where I am. Alone, vulnerable, behind a palm tree. More like a palm leaf at this point.

He leaves the rock to visit the other side, the one with the cave that contains the treasure map. I helped him complete the match with only two treasures, so he should be able to grab it now.

All entities of the game have now gathered on his ship. All except for me.

Sweettooth returns soon, but still leaves me alone. He stands on the bow and looks at me with an expression so sad it instantly brings me to tears.

"It be a gamble, Wildebyte."

"*What?* Hey! Save me! SAVE ME!"

Holding the treasure map, his ship finally agrees to get unstuck and leave the shores. They all sail away, and I helplessly watch them go.

He's leaving me behind!

An eraser scrapes my gun barrel.

Then it whimpers, shrinks to a near invisible size, and zooms away. All other erasers do the same, as if called off by an angry master.

The sun rises once more on Pirate Pound—now missing half its content.

But who or what saved us?

GODS DON'T PLAY LEVEL 3

The first one I see is Ad Brad. But surely that selfish entity wouldn't put all that effort into saving—no, wait, it's still selfish. He probably just wants the game to continue so he can show more *ads*.

"Coooooould I interest you in an eraser-eraser? Looks like you need it."

I glare at him. "The player wants to Uninstall. What makes you think they won't just press the button again?"

Brad frowns. "I know nothing about an uninstall. I just arrived here."

"You didn't save us?"

"Of course not. You have any idea how much *money* that would cost me? *And nobody likes burning money, so get insurance from—*"

"Yeah, yeah."

Sweettooth returns to the beach, of which only half the chunks remain. The return of several items allows me to move again and visit him.

"Hey!" I yell at him. I tried to hide my anger, but it exploded at the pirate all the same. "You were going to leave me behind! Why not take me with you!?"

Sweettooth studies the map in his hands. It shows a path from one end to the other, passing through numerous islands. Only the first two stops, on the first island, have been colored in. The remaining levels are gray and unvisited.

"As I said, it be a gamble. I knew they'd come save us if you were in danger."

"Well I don't *like* being gambled! You were just going to Gamewalk out of here!"

Sweettooth snarls, almost ripping the map apart. "I *can't* Gamewalk anymore!"

What?

Thinking back on my time here, I realize I never missed Sweettooth for a while. He never seemed gone, except perhaps the first time we ran out of lives. Does that mean …

"That's what Bluetooth stole, isn't it?"

He looks away. "He took my Toffee Treasure. The piece of code that enables me to walk between all the games from the Guild."

I hadn't realized. Sweettooth only ever appeared in Guild games; he can't move to games from other developers.

Grocery Empire was a Guild game too, just like Lumbrjax, just like Uptopia Falls. I wonder how Lulu is doing now. I would love to see her again and play her game once more. Better times. Less lonely times.

If you want to know what I'm talking about, I recommend you read the earlier book in this story called *Rulebreaker Recipes*.

See? See how weird it is to advertise another story halfway this story?

"There it is again," I say. "The Guild. Always *the Guild*. Tell me—"

"No, no, no! We don't be talking about the Guild!"

If I had feet, I would stomp the floor or crush something underneath my boots. "I can't work with you if you don't tell me anything! I thought ... I just thought ..."

"You promised me you'd fix the game," Sweettooth says. "It very much be broken at the moment. We be Gamewalking together if you keep your promise, aye. Until then, you be a virus in my game and not worthy of joining the Guild."

I'm tempted to just tell him to sink himself and stalk off. But all the brave thoughts in the world can't battle the loneliness in my heart.

"Fine! Fine. Watch me fix your game. Don't leave without me."

"I would never," Sweettooth says with a slight grin. "Watch you, I mean. I be having better things to do."

"Hmpf."

We both swap away from each other in opposite directions.

I visit the Codeheart to quickly set that number 2 back to 3. The Player was quite clear about the game being way too easy. Now that I know the exact coordinates and exact piece of code, I am in and out before any remaining mini-pirates can tackle me.

I continue moving until I reach the Level Ship, the one that drops items into the level map. Earlier, I completely removed any restrictions on level generation. This meant that it just dropped items randomly and didn't care how hard or easy it was.

Now I realize that is too unpredictable. The game isn't won or lost on skill—it just depends on how lucky you are with how the items are placed. So either the Player is bored or they are frustrated, both of which might lead to an Uninstall.

So I touch the ship and look inside its code. Hmm. I shouldn't have just ripped out all the restrictions. Lesson learned.

It takes me a while to find a link to that piece of code I say in the Codeheart earlier: `checkNeighborsOfItem`. It's next to some piece of code labeled `countTotalMatches`.

Maybe I could ... check if the level has a balanced difficulty? By checking how many matches it has?

A familiar scuttling noise enters this game. Out of the corner of my eye, I see my Graphics Mover. They currently resemble a ghost if it were from a painting by Van Gogh. And I'm surprised I remember that name from the real world, and also hopeful this might mean *more* memories are returning.

Be quick now. I want to speak with her.

And I'm still a little scared Sweettooth leaves me behind anyways.

I tap into that connection and tell the game to only accept a level if there are between 5 and 10 possible matches. The Player has options, but not too many. So check all items, count all matches, use that number.

What then? If the number is greater than 5 and lower than 10, great, keep going. Otherwise …

I fuzz about with the spheres and the tracks over which they race. I break one of them into two, splitting the path like a tree branching. I must admit I have no clue what I'm doing, but I manage to loop the path back to the start. *If there are too few or too many matches, go back to the start and reload the level.*

That last one is more of a guess. I tell the Level Ship to just fly across the entire level again and hope this does the job.

I leave the ship and swap towards the Native Entities.

"There's the troublemaker," the Memory Police says. "Who would be making no more trouble if we had been too slow in saving them."

"Wait—*you* saved us?"

"Barely, darling," the Graphics Mover says. "We noticed the game uninstalling, realized you were still in here, saw you were just … sitting and doing nothing about it."

"So we called it off. Pretended something went wrong. A deadly sin for Ludra, but …"

I grin and poke at his pincer. "Come on. Admit it. You like me."

"We still need you, darling," they state more bluntly.

The Camera enters the game. When it sees the pirate map in Sweettooth's hands, the worn-down paper suddenly grows five times as large, as if it's an inflatable map. It takes all the Player's attention.

"I believe unlocking the campaign has regained some interest in this game," the Police states, walking away. "If you mess it up again, I might not be able to save you. You're not even *paying* me much for the privilege!"

"I don't know how money works in Ludra!"

Ad Brad walks by and laughs at me. "*Uuuuuncertain about your financial stability? Buy a lottery ticket and hope the problem solves itself!*"

"Why is nobody telling me how it works? Then I can generate money and actually pay for stuff."

Brad shakes their head. "Wouldn't want competition."

He continues walking and enters Sweettooth's ship. Why is he coming with us? Does this game make him that much profit?

The Player has studied the map and figured out they need to sail to Level 3. Which they want to play, so they do. They're preparing to leave, which means I'm almost alone on the beach, with just the Graphics Mover watching me with those kind eyes. They currently look like a lopsided ghost from a child's drawing.

"Could you … could you stay with me in the games?" I hear myself ask.

The ghost seems surprised, amused even. "Are hundreds of entities and games not enough for you, darling?"

"Nobody can actually stay with me as I cross games. And except for Outsiders, they are all just … code. Numbers on a device. It doesn't feel real. I feel …"

"Alone?"

I nod and look at them with hopeful eyes.

"We'd love to keep an eye on you at all times, Wildebyte. And as you noticed, we kind of do. You are smart, you are fast, you are like magic. Such a powerful being Ludra has never seen."

Then the Mover crushes my hope.

"But we can't spend the resources to just have Native Entities travel and play with you. We are also very powerful beings required to run this device. Well, unless you have piles of money."

"Then *tell me* how to—"

"But that's not the biggest issue," they say. They float, and I swap, to Sweettooth's ship. Almost everybody is on it.

Sweettooth sticks out his hand to help me board it, which is a nice gesture, but feels weird considering it's unnecessary. Boarding is just another swap with an item already on the ship; in this case a barrel that I hope doesn't contain anything crucial. Because now it will stay behind on the beach.

The ship still has the same statistics, displayed on the hull in thick wooden symbols. *Current real time* and *last time played*. The number of lives, at a precarious 1. And a lot of zeroes that would track our score while playing.

I'm mostly interested by the clear mentions of the *Guild* or the *GGT*. They appear hundreds of times in slightly different fonts, as if somebody was desperate to sign the ship and show it was theirs.

The Graphics Mover studies me with sad eyes.

"Could a god and their peasants be friends? Would a god waste time playing level 3?"

I frown. "Wait. Which one of us is the god in this metaphor?"

"You tell me."

The Mover waves goodbye.

As I wave back, reeling from her words, my form changes again. I turn into a Pirate. Not Sweettooth, not Bluetooth, but one of those smaller and weaker Pirates that protected the Codeheart.

We leave the beach to sail the seas.

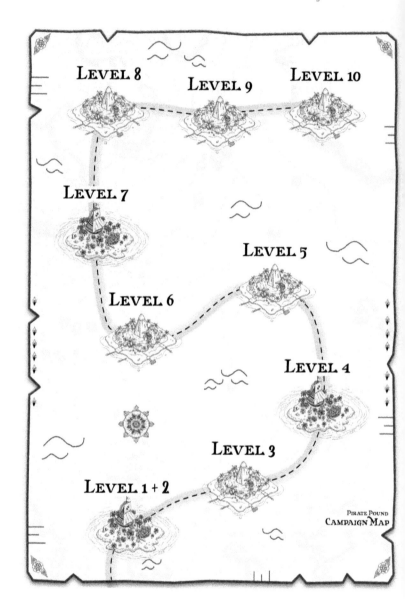

LEVEL 8
LEVEL 9
LEVEL 10
LEVEL 7
LEVEL 5
LEVEL 6
LEVEL 4
LEVEL 3
LEVEL 1 + 2

PIRATE POUND
CAMPAIGN MAP

A Hint of Friendship

I wrongfully assumed the first island was the prettiest place I'd ever seen. Because I hadn't seen the second island yet.

The palm trees are higher here. The lush vegetation shimmers like golden treasure. There is an actual *harbor*, although it's just some wooden planks in a cove for now.

I suspect the next island to have an even larger harbor, even more nature, even better beach. With magical extra-soft sand or dreamy clouds or something.

The Player is equally awed, giving us some time to take it all in and get settled. Then they want to play again.

The Level Ship flies overhead. I hold my breath as it drops the items in neat stacks, forming a bigger grid than the previous two levels. I hope my modifications didn't ruin anything.

They didn't.

I did something right! I did something right!

Sweettooth nods appreciatively. The level always has enough matches, but never too many. Sometimes the Player waits for that hint to come through—a few white circles to show them a possible move—and sometimes they don't need or want that.

I feel actual *fun* returning to the player. I look at myself, now in pirate form. This is the moment, I can feel it. Slowly but surely I will find my match in Sweettooth, just two pirates who will Gamewalk to many game adventures.

As I am not an item anymore, I don't participate in the level. I can watch it from the side, move around it, try to find matches myself.

There's a new item.

Some items are put *inside a glass bottle.* Like a message in a bottle, but now that message can also be a parrot, or, you know, an entire ship. I eagerly await the Player's first usage of such an item.

When they do, I am shocked.

No, literally. It creates a small *explosion*, including an animation where the item breaks out of its glass case. This explosion also removes and scores the surrounding items.

The Player happily creates several explosions, but I already see they won't clear the level. They have way too few points—only a hundred—due to some mediocre swaps at the start.

The error message plays and our final life is taken. Not this again.

But wait! Ad Brad jumps between us and offers the Player to watch an advertisement in return for a life. The Player instantly takes the offer.

Brad waves their hands as if conjuring a spell. His eyes project his marketing film into the sky. Like superman, but instead of shooting killing lasers from his eyes, he has … marketing beams with false promises? Equally dangerous, perhaps.

"*Looove to play games? What if we told you there was a way to turn your entire life into a game! Sign up for the Mixware program and maybe YOU will be the lucky—*"

My first instinct is to tackle Brad and stop the ad. Mixware! The people with their broken science that put me in this device in the first place! I'd rather feel like dying again than hear another thing from Mixware or the researchers.

But what if this advertisement actually convinces the Player? I would have a buddy in this device!

No, that's wrong. It's terrible to be forced inside Ludra. I shouldn't wish that upon any Player.

I simply let the ad play its course, including very sunny images of their headquarters, and loads of examples of mobile games. It feels exceptionally strange. I have actually *been* inside some of the footage they show in the ad.

How are they even getting away with this? Shouldn't the whole world be angry at them for—no, the whole world *doesn't know*. The only one who could tell the world that they put living beings inside devices without a secure way to get them out … is me. Stuck in here.

For all everyone knows, Mixware is just a really cool program that you want to join. No worse than an advertisement for an addictive game or sugary sweet.

Brad smiles, holding a new stack of Data Doubloons in their hands.

"I can't keep saving your behinds, though," his very average face speaks in a very average voice. "The code doesn't allow too many ads in a short period of time. The advertisers fear you might abuse their system! Next life lost is lost."

He doesn't care the slightest bit about that fact. Nor about the content of the ads he displays. He starts counting his coins in a loud voice, to make sure everyone hears he now has 10 more money.

Sweettooth and I lock gazes.

"Perhaps," he says, "a little help be doing no harm, aye?"

"Yes. The sooner we get to Bluetooth and get your Toffee Treasure, the sooner we can Gamewalk *together.*"

Sweettooth doesn't walk away or shut me down. I see progress.

The Player retries level 3. It seems the game itself also decided that more help was needed.

Before the Player even had time to *think*, to look at the level, it already flashes a hint. Not even a good hint. Swapping that would barely solve anything.

The hints are *insistent*. They also make noise now: a sound effect of a pirate saying "swap me, aye!"

The Player waits another few frames, and the entire item starts *flashing*. Soon, that hint is the only thing anyone can see or hear.

Of course the Player follows the hint and performs that swap.

Frustrated, I insert myself into the level. Sweettooth stays on the outside. He seems unable to enter the game, perhaps because he's twice as tall as all the other items.

"The ship top left!" he yells to me. "That be a better match!"

The hint wants something else. A few parrots next to me flash bright and talk over each other to "swap them". The Player immediately follows the hint.

The next hint is similarly insistent and similarly bad. What's *that* swap going to solve? The items are right next to me, teasing me, telling me how *great* it would be to swap them.

"I know! I know! But I don't *want* to swap you!" I say.

But of course the Player is drawn to the hint and immediately executes it.

"Four rows down, two to the left," Sweettooth tells me. "Quick!"

I swap around the level according to his instructions. This is working much better than I thought. Sweettooth with the good ideas, and I execute without hesitation. What a collaboration! Maybe that's just how it should be. One entity should be in command and the others follow.

The renewed energy from this thought helps me race around the map. This places me in-between a bunch of items inside glass bottles.

"Hey!" I yell, looking at the Camera. "Swap ME! ME ME ME!"

The Player can't hear me, of course. Previous games confirmed that time and time again. But I hope the animations and special effects draw their attention. If not that, they must be confused what my pirate body is doing in the wrong place.

It works.

The Player swaps *me* with a treasure chest inside a glass bottle.

Explosions, explosions, explosions.

This was a terrible idea.

A rough hand yanks me away from the explosions. I land outside of the level bounds, held in place by Sweettooth, and watch half the level clearing itself and scoring a gazillion points. That's, like, way more than a hundred.

Another new rule appears. We hadn't seen it before because the Player hadn't reached this far, but now they are on track to clear level 3 easily.

Some items now have a *sword* stuck through them. The sword either points horizontally or vertically.

"I don't know about you," I say, my voice still shocked from being in the middle of the explosions. "But those items seem shiny and special."

Sweettooth laughs. "I do be agreeing. One more time?"

"Just tell me where to go."

I insert myself into the level again. The Player keeps following the hints. I had hoped my actions showed them there are *better* moves, but instead it reinforced they have to follow the commands.

Once inside a stack, I lose all sense of direction again. Being inside a level, you just can't tell what's going on around you or what the best match would be. It's like having vertigo while being glued to a glass window.

"Five to the left, three down," Sweettooth yells. He also uses his knives to point to the right location.

The Player already touched an item suggested by the hints system.

"NO! FOLLOW ME!"

I end up where the pirate wanted me, above a treasure chest with a horizontal sword through it. The Player takes their thumb off of their screen and places it on me again.

We swap.

I am happy the chest is below me, not next to me.

Because once swapped, the chest clears the entire *row*. That's what they do. Once swapped, they instantly remove all items in the direction at which their sword pointed. Or rather gave them all a one-way ticket to that Sweethaven. A place I don't intend to go.

Clearing this many items shot our score through the roof. We already made it, but the Player has a few moves left and uses them to … follow bad hints again.

Oh well.

I let Sweettooth pull me out of there, back to safety. We watch from a distance as the level is finished.

"That be impressive work," he says.

"Nah, I had help."

The treasure map glows brightly and reveals the path to level 4, on the next island. We jump into the ship and set sail immediately.

    Wait a minute—shouldn't this have taken our last life? Why are we all still awake?

Friendship Goals

As we approach the next island, Sweettooth nudges my shoulder. He gives me the treasure map and sits down next to me.

"The map goes a lot further," he says, "but Bluetooth's hideout is only at level 10. I be sure more levels were planned. I be less sure the Guild actually made them."

"As long as we help the Player," I say with a smile, "we might be there before nightfall."

Sweettooth grins. "Be liking the optimism, aye, but levels be getting harder and harder."

He finally looks relaxed. Calm. Enjoying the soft breeze and the open sea. Guess that's the benefit of the lives system suddenly just … stopping. You realize how much stress and anxiety it gives you at all times.

"How do you know that?" I ask. Bluetooth's hideout isn't on the map, and level 10 doesn't look much different than the others around it.

"We've fought many times before."

"Unsuccessfully, I see?"

"Bluetooth has an Unmatchable Underworld," he says. "A sort of cave or tunnel system that be *impossible* to match or break into. They be hiding my Toffee Treasure and your Lost Memory there, aye be sure."

I frown. "Nothing is every *truly* impossible for the Wildebyte to break into."

"Glad we have you along for the ride," he says, grabbing my shoulders. "Even if it took a Lost Memory for you to join us."

I kind of wish he hadn't reminded me. Every Lost Memory is an important memory from my life in the real world. Another puzzle piece to tell me where I come from and what I'm missing now—and maybe a way out of Ludra. I look away to hide the tears.

"Are you … ready to talk about the Guild now—"

"No talking about the Guild yet!"

"Ugh. Can you at least answer other questions?" I point at the two times on the boat. "Why does this game track the current time and last time played?"

Sweettooth flashes his golden tooth, moving his hands wildly as he explains. "Did you really think the game keeps calculating, every second, if five hours have passed and a new life must be grown? Did you think the game stops regenerating lives if you close it?"

"Well, yeah, kind of."

"No! It be much simplerrrr, aye!" He points at the numbers as if he still had his sword. "The game simply remembers the time you last lost a life. Whenever the Player logs back in, it be comparing that time with the current time. That's how it knows how many lives the player should've received in the mean time."

"Ah. So if there are ten hours between *now* and when the player received their previous life, it adds two lives immediately?"

That's how games can keep things going. How they regenerate lives or coins or whatever over a long time without needing to be turned on or played. Or connected to the internet, which is what I *think* those squiggly lines do.

"You not be so empty-skulled after all."

"You have an odd way of calling somebody *really smart*," I jest.

He gets up as we approach the new island. As expected, it has a bigger harbor with two locations for ships to anchor. It's larger and has a high pillar of stones in the center, which holds some numbers and images I can't read from this distance.

As we step onto the beach, side by side, the purpose of the pillar reveals itself.

The game has received different *objectives*. All the previous levels had the same goal—reach at least X points—but this level has a different goal.

We win if we manage to *remove a hundred treasure chests.*

Brad joins us once he finally stops counting his money.

"Very good, very good," he says. "This looks like a *very tough level.* Will need to show many ads, *and as we say at the research station, the more the merrier!*"

The Player starts playing, but mostly ignores the new goal. They just follow the hints and score points, which leads to only a mere thirty chests removed by the time they inevitably fail.

Sweettooth and I mostly let it happen, to see what the lives system would do. It's still broken, or at least disabled. The Player realizes they have infinite lives and just tries again and again.

"Dear Wildebyte," Sweettooth says. He actually addressed me. More progress! "Could you perhaps tap into the hint system and turn it off? Or at least make it be less flashy-annoyo?"

"On it, captain! Though never use the word flashy-annoyo again, please!"

"Coooooould I interest you in an English dictionary for only—"

"Shut up, Brad."

They don't seem insulted. In fact, they seem used to being shut up or ignored—and somehow I feel they will never change their ways because of that.

I climb back into the level and try to reach the items that are currently part of the hint. I'm too slow the first time. The second time, I manage to touch one of the white circles around a treasure chest, *before* the Player inevitably follows the hint.

Stop it. Stop giving hints. No more hints.

I send it all the thoughts and commands I can think of. That doesn't work, of course. Computers don't listen to your feelings. After some effort, though, the code reveals itself to be simple.

A long list of transparent tiles floats in front of me. Like a conveyor belt moving copies of items on the map. This list comes from the code of the Level Ship: it produces this list of *possible matches* when checking the map at the start.

An anchor lowers from the flying ship, from a frayed dark-brown rope. It *hooks* into the first item on this conveyor belt and then pulls it up. Once it's back at the flying ship, the new hint is determined.

Alright, so. To give a hint, it just picks the very first match from that list and draws some circles around it. Immediately. That's all it does.

Were the developers that afraid of losing any player due to being too difficult?

Ugh, they couldn't even write code to pick a *random* match from the list! Or a *good* one! It's just always the first one. The first match from this conveyor belt of possible matches.

Now that I know this, I see how to abuse it. I simply put the match that I think is great into the list *at the start*. So it will always pick that and show that hint.

As I'm about to ask Sweettooth what to insert, an item starts talking to me.

"Please just let me go to Sweethaven," a parrot says. "Please!"

"Fine. I'll let this hint stand."

As I turn around, more items suddenly want to speak with me.

"Why do you work together with him?" one asks.

"You're not like him. Why are you doing this?" another asks.

"Can't you just leave us alone? Manipulating systems has never been good," another states.

I raise my hands to silence them all. The Player is confused just long enough to let me finish speaking. "What are you talking about? Thanks to *us* we're now at level 4."

"Thanks to you. Sweettooth is a *monster*."

"You're just trying to annoy me," I say, waving at Sweettooth. He smiles and waves back, though looking a bit confused. "If that were true, why didn't any of you tell me before? You had plenty of chances!"

"Because we were too afraid of him then," the parrot states solemnly.

he Player decided they wanted to follow this hint and the parrots vanish to Sweethaven.

"Isn't it suspicious," I hear from a compass with eyes. "That your Lost Memory was stolen at the same time, by the exact same person, as the thing stolen from Sweettooth?"

"Yes. And also very much an accident. He hid it in the same place as his Toffee Treasure."

"Why hide it at all? Isn't that Lost Memory yours?"

I shake my head. "No, no, you're trying to upset me. Not going to happen!"

I dance away from them until I can't hear their lies. The closer I get to Sweettooth, though, the fewer items are willing to speak up.

"You tapped into the hint system?" Sweettooth asks expectantly.

"Yup. You tell me the best match, I tell that to the player … very insistently."

He grins as he points out the first one. A glass bottle and a sword through a compass. I quickly figure out their locations and insert those as the first hint.

Indeed, the system happily hooks the anchor into that suggestion, lifts it back up, and then beams it to the player.

They follow it and create a chain of explosions along an entire stack—or column, in the eyes of the Player.

Points upon points rain on us. But most importantly, that stack had loads of treasure chests. Sweettooth knows what he's doing, at least. We're nearing a hundred chests, the goal of the level.

"We make a great team!" I yell from the top of a safe stack. "A dream team!"

"High-rate pirates!" he yells back.

"Besters matchers!"

He indicates a nice swap at the bottom left. I hint it to the Player. They follow.

That will do the trick. Two matches at the same time, one using four items, and a bottle explosion bring us to exactly a hundred treasure chests removed.

Confetti, sparkles, unnecessarily loud sound effects. I tumble back down to Sweettooth as the level dissolves itself. It hands loads of bonus points to the Player for finishing with 10 moves left, something the game calls a *Pirate Plunderrrr!*

On to the next island. On to level 5.

But the comments from the items eat at me. Maybe it's a mistake. They are probably lying about Sweettooth and just trying to make me angry.

But I feel like our bond is good enough now that I can ask him a tougher question.

"Sweettooth, be honest with me. Did you give my Lost Memory away to Bluetooth on purpose?"

Blocked Passage

Sweettooth might be secretive, or rather *mysterious*, but he is no liar. Maybe that's why he distrusts me so much. I can't even count the number of lies I already told since entering Ludra.

"Aye did," Sweettooth says. "I be sure you would never help if you had no skin in the game."

"No what?"

"If I be giving you Lost Memory for free, all that time ago, would you be here now?"

"Yes! Yes, yes, yes," I say, exasperated. "I'm here to help you, because I want to Gamewalk with you!"

Sweettooth looks away. "You know I can only follow into Guild games?"

"Fine. You've taken over half the device anyway."

"Oh no, I'm not *part* of the Guild. I *work* for the Guild."

"How is that different?"

He makes the face he always makes when he realizes he talked about the Guild—and you're not supposed to talk about the Guild.

"I forgive you," I say in my softest voice. Just stay calm, just talk about it, you are still a dream team. "I

113

understand why you did it. Just don't hide things from me again."

"Aye," Sweettooth agrees. "Let's kick some Bluetooth butt before nightfall, aye?"

The sea has different plans.

Brad pushes us aside to stand on the bow. He points at sheets of *ice* blocking our passage. The wind turns freezing cold and the sky more gray than blue.

"That be a surprise. Ice sheets around tropical islands."

The ship bumps into them—and breaks. Part of the bow splinters and sinks into the water. Brad barely jumps into the safety of the sail.

Sweettooth immediately lowers anchor to prevent any further damage. The ship will sail, but it won't look as pretty. And maybe steering will become an issue.

And also sailing.

In his terror, Brad rips apart the sails as he tries to hang on. What used to be one white sheet now turns into three vertical stripes of cloth, falling slowly.

Brad's eyes turn on and beam an advertisement, out of his control.

You love playing games, kid? Then try out Palace Run! Play this game, reach level 3, jump into the bushes on the right, crawl to a hidden exit, wait for the power beam to hit you, and you should have an experience you haven't had in a long time!

What?

Sweettooth yells at me to help repair his ship and destroy the ice. He isn't making any progress on both goals. But I barely hear him, processing the content of that advertisement.

"That is ... needlessly specific."

Brad's eyes turn off again. He barely gets money for this, as he slides down the mast—now lacking a sail—as if he's asleep.

"Who told you to display that ad?" I demand. "Who paid you for it?"

Brad shakes his head. "Can't tell. Privacy laws."

"*Really?*" I run to the other side, trying to snatch the three patches of what used to be our sail.

This must be the researchers. They sent ads to all the games in this device, hoping one would find me. They want me to visit a very specific place and ... wait for them to extract me?

"Please please please, I beg you." Brad isn't interested in begging. Of course not. He wants money and power, nothing else. "I will tell all the other games to use *you* for displaying ads, if you tell me who gave you this ad and why."

In my haste, I completely fail to grab our sails. They drift towards the water, like parachutes holding no payload, leaving the ship with nothing to catch wind.

Brad looks *interested* in my proposal.

"At least repeat the ad to me. I have to memorize all that."

Palace Run. Level 3. What then?

He shakes his way too polished, boyish head. "Pay me or nothing happens."

I turn to Sweettooth. "Is *Palace Run* a game by the Guild?"

"Never heard of it! Now could you please—"

As the three patches of our sail hit the water, they form a three-in-a-row. They vanish in a shower of sparks and congratulations.

That's normal. What isn't normal, is the fact that this match also *melted* some of the ice nearby. Sweettooth couldn't do it, not with a thousand kicks. But now the ship can finally move forward again.

We race to collect three objects of the same type. All the *items* traveling with us are not so eager to be used, as matching now would send them to Bitterhell or Salty Shores or whatever the opposite of Sweethaven is.

We manage to find three barrels, which we use to melt the next patch of ice. Repeating the process several times, we finally reach the next island.

An island *made* of ice. Besides this crucial difference, it's identical to the previous one. Same size, same vegetation, same Codeheart location.

Even the stone pillars in the center—showing the objective—are exactly the same. Including their broken parts and chipped stones.

The only difference is the objective itself. This level has another new objective: *clear all the Curses.*

The Level Ship attracts all items, then flies by to fill the new level. Some items, however, become *cursed* shortly after being added.

Their colors change to a darker tone, offset by a bright alarming glow around them. They grow nasty bumps and bulges in their skin. Like they're … sick?

No. As I study the sickness for longer, I realize it's not attached to the items. It's attached to the *location.*

How do I know? Because there's another thing that *does* attach to items: ice. Some of them get trapped in a large chunk of ice, which forbids them from moving at all.

The code isn't even smart enough to recognize that. The first hint it gives tells the Player to swap a frozen item, which it *can't.* Whatever the Guild is, they can't program very well. Maybe that James is the *only* programmer they have!

Sweettooth, Brad and I look at each other. We can already guess how this works, right?

At their commands, I insert different matches into the hint system. The Player follows, though with a noticeable delay.

When we match three treasure chests, a frozen item *next to it* melts!

Similarly, when we match an item on a cursed location, the curse is removed from the location. Some spots are extra cursed though—indicated by an even brighter light and sicker appearance—and need to do this multiple times.

Working together, we focus on healing and unfreezing, instead of scoring many points. The special items, such as those with a sword through them, come in especially handy. To clear spots that are hard to reach in the corner, or spots that—due to our bad luck—just don't generate matches for many moves in a row.

With effort, we help the player clear level 5 on the first try.

"Great job, dream team!"

"I'm not part of this!" Brad says grumpily. "Now I don't get any opportunities to display my ads! The Player might *miss the best offers of their lifetime* and *cheap deals while supplies last!*"

Sweettooth playfully pushes them aside as we already return to the ship. "Aye, this empty-skulled being was just yelling random locations to hope you mess up."

"Good thing I don't trust that sleek money-hungry entity," I say, glaring at Brad with full intensity.

Sweettooth grunts. "Nobody does. Still Brad be *everywhere* on this device."

"Yes, yes, you all hate me, great."

I notice the slightest chink in their armor. A brief sad face and slumped shoulders, until they return to their overly happy salesman look.

Night falls in-game and we travel to the next island.

Sweettooth hums a song. A pretty one. Surprisingly, his coarse voice makes it sound even better, instead of sounding forced and like a dying cat.

After a while, it turns into a proper sea shanty. A beautiful uplifting melody easily carries across the waves, surely reaching as far as Bluetooth's hideout, as Sweettooth sings while repairing the mast.

"*When I was a young boy, they tied me down. With rules and restrictions, a life with a frown. They told me to stay home and forget the waves. But aye, aye aye aye, could never live that way.*"

"*I stole my first ship from a fisherman slow,*" I chime in. How do I know these words? Is this a popular sea shanty from the real world? Sweettooth adjusts and sings the melody in a second, lower voice. "*The Police chasing, shipwrecked, as I smile on my bow. Yes the life of a pirate fits me like rubber boots. And aye, aye aye aye, will have nothing to lose.*"

Smiling, I stand up, eager to start the next refrain that I also know by heart.

But Sweettooth coughs and stops singing.

"You can't sing. Your voice be like stone crying on sand. Another reason why we shouldn't Gamewalk together."

Ouch.

Sweettooth walks away. He hums, more softly now, as he studies the map.

I decide to visit Brad and sit with him. Our backs lean against the mast, shoulders touching.

"I know how it feels," I start. "To be hated by everyone."

"Feelings don't matter to me," he recites robotically. "Only money."

"The trick is to, you know, *not* say things like that and live that way."

"You only say that because you never had piles and piles of money, and the responsibility of half the world on your shoulders."

When he turns his face to look at me, he suddenly looks like a woman with frizzy hair in an oversized lab coat—one of the Mixware researchers.

Shapes and Sizes

Brad grabs my shoulders. I wriggle out of his grip. He grabs me again, but there is no aggression there, no malicious intent. He desperately wants to be *touching* me, but he isn't killing me or anything.

Hey, kid, long time no talk.

That voice. That researcher voice! It's back in my head! It's joined by the familiar speech bubbles and radio signals floating around me.

The shock helps me evade Brad's grip once more and keep my distance.

"*It's your lucky day!*" Brad says. "The Mixware team has found a way to get you out of this device. *In these troubled times,* they are still willing to risk it all to help you back to your real life."

"Yeah, sure. I can't trust you."

Brad keeps his smile wide and bright. "They told me you'd say this. So they also gave me ..."

His eyes light up and show another ad. This one starts with a logo that looks official, like it's from the king or ... the President? Then it shows a mobile phone, and another, and another, before playing a deafening error sound and displaying a cross through them.

"_The President has written a law proposal that will BAN all phones or other addictive digital handheld devices. Think about it! You'll never play games like these again! Let government know what you think and fight this proposal at—"

Our ship arrives at the pretty harbor on the next island, which should contain level 6. Brad stumbles and the ad flickers, but it was mostly finished anyway.

"They're planning to outlaw all phones in the real world?" I say in disbelief. "And destroy them, I presume?"

Brad nods, a hint of fear in his shifting pupils. Ah, so he does understand that no money in the world would save his existence then.

"The *Mixware Corporation* wanted me to tell you that your time in Ludra might be cut short any time. They realize you don't trust them. But the risk of going to *Palace Run* and trying their extraction method is far smaller than the risk if you wait and do nothing."

I look over my shoulder. Sweettooth is already swapping around to explore the new island, though his movement seems hampered. Not all items are eager and happy to help him anymore.

The temptation is high. Just find and visit Palace Run and maybe I'm back in my real life in a day or two.

But Sweettooth can't follow, as it's not a "Guild Game".

And this is exactly why nobody trusts *me* or wants to stay with *me*.

"No. I promised to fix this game and complete the mission. And I stick to my promises. I will come to Palace Run when I'm ready."

Brad is stunned. "They can't keep this opportunity open if *all phones are destroyed!* You see that, right? *Tired of not seeing things? Get your ultracool glasses from—*"

"I see that. I also see other things now."

The Camera arrives, meaning the Player arrives, to play level 6. At first glance, I don't see anything special. The shape and bounds of the level are different, but I find no new items or blocking locations.

Though some stacks have a weird image at their top or bottom. Not quite an item, not a living entity, but something like a ... gate?

At first, I thought the objective was to clear 10 ships again. Then I realize this is a really low number. And that this specific ship, with these colors and sails, isn't even in the level!

Guided by Sweettooth, I abuse the hint system again to steer the Player to the best matches.

It takes a few matches before I see what the gate is doing. Those special ships *appear* through the gate at the top. And once they do, the gate at the bottom opens.

"We must bring these ships down!" I yell at Sweettooth. "We win if 10 of them sail through the gates at the bottom!"

He takes a while to realize what I mean, then nods and changes his tactic. Now the game feels like steering the ships. The pillar also tells me this is the *FLOW* objective. With each match, we want to remove as many items as possible *below* ships, so that they sail downwards and leave the level quickly.

The Player's interest renews, as does my own. They were responding more and more slowly to the hints, but now they pick up speed again.

Only a few more special ships to go. Sweettooth starts joking about "being in the flow". I tell him that I "ship this level".

Until we create two matches at the same time and are in for a surprise. Instead of entirely going away, one of the items—which used to be a normal palm tree—is *replaced* by a palm tree in a glass bottle.

Why? We had multiple matches in one turn before, why is this one—

"That be a T-shape!" Sweettooth tells me. I believe him, because he has a better view of the whole map. "The one match be horizontal, the other be vertical, so together it created a T-shape. That be the difference."

I freeze. I never even thought about it.

Earlier, I learned how the matching works. It starts with each item, then tries to "infect" its neighbors of the same type, until it can't infect further. I never realized that this wasn't the entire code—it also needed to check if those items were all *on the same line.*

In previous levels, a match was only valid if all items had the same horizontal coordinate (X) or the same vertical coordinate (Y). Otherwise you could just match 3 items in a *corner* or in a *zigzag* or any shape! Which would be ugly and way too easy.

With this level, though, other shapes for the group are suddenly allowed.

"Try something else! Like an L shape!" I tell Sweettooth.

He instructs me where to go. Before I know it, a group of treasure chests is replaced by a single candy with a sword through it.

Alright, so these special shapes also give you a special item in return. Which you can use for even bigger explosions and more items cleared in the next turns.

"Let's do a 2 by 2 square!" Sweettooth says.

"Great idea!"

I have to wait a while. The Player is responding *slowly* now. They might even be considering other moves besides what we hint, which I'd normally like, but not while we're trying to speedrun through these levels to reach Bluetooth at level 10.

Once we make our 2 by 2 square, we are indeed rewarded with a new special item. It's just a black silhouette, however, as if we made it too quickly and will only unlock it at the next level. That's also why it refuses to match or be moved.

This makes the Player react even more slowly.

Only three turns left. Only one ship left to flow to an exit. Sweettooth has already found the right move, I've been hinting it a while, but the Player just—

They do a different move.

A terrible move.

Why!?

We scramble to make up for it. But the next turn never comes. The Player waits, and waits, and waits, and then just *leaves* the level without completing it.

Sweettooth lowers his eyebrows. "Aye, that be the danger of *not* having a lives system. They don't be caring anymore about completing each attempt."

The level quickly dissolves. Everyone is a little disappointed and our great highscore just evaporates. Did something come up? Maybe they were interrupted? No, that would just mean we had to wait for longer. They explicitly *shut us down.*

Sweettooth looks lost in thought. "This isn't good. I need to check the social messages, maybe the Player has told their friends something."

He gives me a final smile. "Try not to destroy everything, aye?"

Then he swaps away to the other side of the island. This island looks identical to the very first one, so he probably assumes his special cave—the one handling messages between friends—to be in the exact same location.

Wait a minute. He just left me alone with his ship, and all the items, and everything! Finally he *trusts* me.

I can't stop smiling and telling all the items we're a dream team.

They want to tell *me* something else.

"Quick! Listen! Before he comes back," a parrot hisses in my ear.

The Wild Wild West

The items crowd around me, as if they seek to capture me. But it doesn't feel suffocating, because I know I can use them to swap away at any time.

"We told you that the lives system wasn't always this way, right?" the parrot starts.

"Yeah, Bluetooth ruined it for—" No, Bluetooth wasn't here to turn off the lives system. Only me, Brad and Sweettooth. And I didn't do it. "You're saying Sweettooth turned it off? But he can't mess with the game code like I can, right?"

"No. But he basically invented the whole thing!" a pirate exclaims, who is similar in appearance to me. "He made the lives system himself, so he controls it entirely."

"The old system gave you 20 lives and you only lost one if you *lost* a level. Then Sweettooth came and changed that to 5. And you lost a life on every attempt. And being out of lives feels like *dying* to all items in the game."

"But … but …" I mumble. "Why not tell me this at the start?"

"He *uses* the lives system to control us," the parrot says. "They don't wash up on shore. He pretends to be this great pirate that works tirelessly, searching the beaches, to find lives for us. But as he explained to you, it's done automatically every time five hours have passed."

I don't want it to be true. But it feels true. All this time, I forgot ... that Sweettooth is a *pirate*. As pirate-y as they come.

"He simply receives the new heart," I mumble, "throws some sand on it, and pretends he found it. And if any of you tell the truth or disobey his commands ..."

They all make a gesture as if crushing a heart and then dying. They only dare speak out because the lives system is gone and they feel *somewhat* safe.

"But then you know Sweettooth can also turn the lives back on whenever he pleases. This is still risky for you!"

"Which is why we are *whispering* while the old pirate is *away*," the parrot says.

Anger boils inside me. He didn't outright lie to me, but he surely held back some of the important facts. He's been ... he's been ... *torturing* these poor items just to keep control of this game and to be seen as the hero.

In my restlessness, I start swapping at random with the group. My eyes are cast down, studying the sandy beach as if every grain of sand is suddenly really interesting, hiding the anger brewing behind my eyes.

What am I going to do? What are *we* going to do?

The only thing I know. Head-on collision, jump in. With help from the items, I *race* to the other side of the island to meet Sweettooth at the cave.

As expected, they are reading social messages sent by the Player.

> **PresidentNotMyDad:** so DONE with this. The game just keeps telling me what to do. Those hints are blinding me. I'm not even playing a game anymore, just following COMMANDS.

> **JumpyFlamingo10:** I'm seriously doubting if we're playing the same game anymore.

> **PresidentNotMyDad:** well I'm NOT playing this STUPID game anymore. It wouldn't even let me UNINSTALL the first time.

> **JumpyFlamingo10:** maybe it's just corrupted or something. My hints are

terrible and only appear if I play really badly. But you have somehow shot to level 6 with global highscores. You have the best score in the world on level 4!!!

PresidentNotMyDad: whatever. I'm deleting.

JumpyFlamingo10: then give the account to me!

The chat is going on right now. I can't wait any longer.

"Sweettooth!" I yell, drawing a scared stance from him. "You have been the one betraying my trust. You turned off the lives system. You are the one that changed it into some terror mechanic in the first place!"

All the items are long gone. He can't possibly find the few items that told me if they're all on different parts of the island now.

"Aye did. And look where it brought us!" he says with a smile. "We're in full control of this game and cruising towards our goal."

"This isn't *good*. I don't want to reach my Lost Memory if it means helping a *criminal*."

"I be a Pirate, Wildebyte. What did you expect?"

I freeze. "You're not even denying it? Not even insulted?"

"I'm insulted you thought I was some do-gooder who be eating his vegetables and praying to god every night. Aye thought you wanted to be friends *because* we shared our appetite for destruction and chaos."

"*What?* Just stop it. All the things you're manipulating or ruining. Stop all of it, or I … I won't be your friend!"

This amuses him. "Fine, then we won't be friends. Good luck finding the exit!"

He's gone.

What did I do?

I thought we'd just have a nice shouting match and then agree to be better and continue. That's how it goes, right? But he doesn't care. He'll just be pirating all over the place whether somebody likes it or not.

Which leaves me alone on an island again.

No Sweettooth. No Player anymore.

I start crying. A lone pirate in the sand, looking out on an empty sea. Even the endless sea feels more full of life than myself. So far into the journey, yet still so far to go. The items can't be my friends. The Native Entities can't stay with me. Even—

Oh broken buttons. There's only one person left for me. It suddenly doesn't matter how much I despise him—I yell his name, unable to move myself until items come near.

Not long after, Brad skips onto the beach, which grows darker under the setting sun.

"So you finally realized most entities are as selfish as me?" he says gleefully. "I told you at the start."

"Why … why can't entities just be friends *because it's nice*? Not because of what we can give each other. Not as a transaction, like buying friendship in a shop. Getting a friend after watching their ad."

"Doooo you want to watch an ad right—"

"No!"

"Sorry. Can't help myself."

Despite my small frame, my pirate form still casts a large shadow over the boyish form of Brad. I feel like a monstrous giant next to that tiny bouncing guy.

"Why can't the Memory Police just give me all the Lost Memories, then help me get out? Why all the secrets about how money works? Why forbid any other entities from Gamewalking? Why be angry whenever I do anything mildly different? *Why all the rules!?*"

Brad laughs. He laughs so hard that he bounces away from me and ends with his face in the sand.

"Rules? *What rules?* Handheld Ludra—on a smartphone—is like the wild wild west. You think our Memory Police is harsh? They're the friendliest, loosest, nicest Native Entity you'll find on any device. We don't even follow the Video Game Code. I'd love to see your face once you get to experience *that. Just as you will love our new product, on sale today while supplies last, so get yours at—*"

"So you're saying I just have to accept all the chaos because it *could be worse?*"

"The Memory Police might be angry. They might threaten. But you're still alive, right? And they interrupted an uninstall—a deadly sin, as they said, going against the User's wishes—just to save you."

Brad is still laughing at me; it feels increasingly deserved. "On other devices, being erased is a huge *protocol* that needs to be followed. There is a vote, there is a process. In here? The Memory Police—and their small children—just walk around with a big eraser dangling from their belt, destroying stuff willy-nilly."

Brad shakes his head. But he is very happy with what he's about to say: "No, Handheld Ludra is chaos squared, rules optional, privacy optional. It's the only way I could make *sooo much money!*"

I'm tempted to ask him to share some of it with me. But I already know the response: "What do I get in return?"

"Though you shouldn't be too hard on Sweettooth," Brad says. "The fact that Ludra has no rules, doesn't mean that his game—or the Guild—doesn't force him to do stuff."

Right. I keep forgetting these entities are just code, programmed to respond to specific situations in specific ways. That's where their character, their dialogue, their animations come from. Maybe I just need to become better at finding the situations that bring the best out of entities in Handheld Ludra.

I touch Brad's shoulders. Immediately, through him, the connection between me and the researchers is restored.

Finally ready to talk? that female voice says.

"You do the talking first. Where are my parents? Does the world know about me and this situation? What is up with the President and his no-phones law?"

Slow down, kid. Even this conversation is dangerous and needs to stay hidden.

"Then do the talking fast."

Can't Stay, Can't Go

The researchers confirm both my biggest hopes and my worst fears. They have no clue where my parents are, but the whole world is looking for them. They promise they are being honest and *have* found a way out through that other game, but they also honestly tell me I might not like the life to which I return.

The no-phones law is up for a vote soon, but they're doing all they can to stop it. That "ad" from Brad was actually from them, broadcast all over the world to inform gamers about it.

I still want to test them. "Okay, so tell me how it works. How does the technology to extract me work?"

That's very complicated science, kid. But the reason we couldn't do the reverse before is probably because your memories and personality were accidentally scattered across the device. That's why we need this new game. It violates a few privacy laws to access the entire device and collect EVERYTHING connected to you. So we can get you back in one piece.

That sounds … sensible? Could it be true?

"And what about the dangers you sent to kill me before?"

A panic move, we must admit.

"A panic move? That's all?"

Don't pretend you haven't almost bricked this device in several panic moves.

"My mistakes don't make your mistakes good."

A long silence. The voice returns more softly.

We really should use this time to talk about more important things.

I hate myself for feeling *relieved* to talk to them. I should be mad until the end of time. I should be plotting my revenge as we speak. Yelling their names and some curses from the highest island, threatening to burn their homes and steal their pets.

But their comfortable voice in my head, a voice from *the real world*, just feels nice.

Until Brad has to leave.

The connection is harshly disrupted, as if waking from a nightmare in cold sweat. He mumbles his apologies.

"Does another game need you right now?"

"No, this game does."

Now I hear the sound effects. They're playing level 6 without me. But seeing how much the Player dislikes the game by now, this probably won't end well.

I have one final idea on how to fix that.

Since Sweettooth left, items have dared come near me again. Thanks to them, I can swap to the Codeheart on this island. In exactly the same location as the first island, with exactly the same shape. They must all be connected, because my modifications stay in the game, no matter where we go.

I swap inside the green shield, ready for another fight with protective pirates. But there are none. There is just *one* pirate, who looks identical to me, who greets me and goes about their business.

Alright. So they weren't angry with *me*, they were angry with *Sweettooth*.

I can touch the heart and look inside its code without issue. We need a way to get the Player to ignore the hints again. To realize they *can* make a different decision, they *can* actually play the game and ignore us. They have a choice, even though it might not seem like it.

My ears keep picking up success or error sound effects from the others retrying level 6. I need to be quick. My best idea appears when I notice the word `delayBeforeTurnAllowed`.

Apparently, there's a half-second delay before the Player is even allowed to swap. A developer comment explains this.

> *Note (@James): To prevent the player accidentally doing a swap they didn't intend,*

> *because their fingers are still on the screen*
> *from the previous one.*

I can raise this number to something far higher. Five seconds. No, ten seconds. The Player has to wait at least ten seconds before doing a move.

This should give them ample time to ignore the hint and make up their own mind!

Satisfied, I find my way back to the beach, looking at the stacks of items from the *back*. That obviously doesn't change a single thing about the game or the map, but it still looks weird because the background *behind* the items is so different.

Not much is happening. The Player is certainly touching items, which is indicated by the item growing slightly larger and getting a glow effect around it. But the 10 second delay means they keep trying to swap and just *nothing happens*.

Yes. Take a deep breath, Player. Think about it. Search a better match, ignore the hint.

They do. A few moments later, they try a different swap. This time, the 10 second delay has passed, so it happens.

This repeats two more times before the Player finally realizes the delay and stops trying to swap items before the timer runs out. They learn quickly— which is also probably why they bore quickly.

The Player is making much smarter moves, ignoring the hints. And still I don't feel more than a smidge of *fun* radiating from the Player. It's mostly boredom, waiting, waiting, waiting until they are … allowed to play the game.

Yeah. This was a mistake.

They finish level 6, prompting cheers from Sweettooth and Brad, and quickly get back into their boat to find the next island.

But the Player is certainly looking for that UNINSTALL button right now.

"Brad! Could you come here, please?" I ask, frozen on the empty beach.

If I tried to climb on the boat, Sweettooth wouldn't actually *stop* me, right? Right? He just did something that I might have done as well to gain control. Maybe I should just forgive him and ask to be his friend again.

But haven't we repeated this loop enough times by now?

"Well alright then, because you said *please*," Brad says jokingly. Once he's within range, I touch his shoulders to speak with the researchers again.

Is that you? Are you back?

"Hey, researchers, forget all I said before. I forgive you. Just … stay with me. Please? Could you return to my head at all times?"

Silence. A long silence.

"Did you hear me? Are you still there?"

Yes.

"Can you do it? Restore the connection without needing Ad Brad?"

Ad Brad? Who is—Oh, you mean the advertising system. Yes, we could.

"So?"

Only if you promise to let us take full control and don't fight us. Otherwise we will lose you all the time and you'll go do your own thing, and we don't have the money or resources to waste on that anymore.

I sigh. Sure, they gave me a choice. But is it really a choice? "We will help you, but only if you become our slave." It's like saying: "We'll save your life, but only if you pay us a million dollars." Or: "Sure you can take the bike, but it will take you seven months to get to your destination."

Some choices aren't actually choices.

Some hints, if too insistent and too prominent, aren't actually mere hints anymore.

That's our problem. That's been our problem the whole time. *We're preventing the player from actually playing the game!*

"You know I will never agree to that," I tell the researchers.

We don't care. It's the only way this will work, so that's our ultimatum.

"Then the answer is no."

Reluctantly, I let go of Brad and tell him not to let me touch him again. I don't want the temptation of those researchers helping me when they'll just let me down again. Unfortunately, we are also no match.

I turn around.

Sweettooth has *left.*

All entities in the game just sailed off to the next island, leaving me behind. Brad doesn't seem panicked. He doesn't need to follow any game rules and will find his own way to catch up.

But what do I have? I'm stuck!

The anger inside me grows to an entirely new level. It might even grow all the way to level 7, because I transform into ... into ...

Tentacles erupt from me. One, two, more, more, until I have eight. My pirate form is long gone, replaced by an octopus.

No, not just an octopus. A huge, scary, monstrous octopus with sharp teeth the size of entire pirate ships.

I have become a *Kraken.*

Roaring, I swap with the water blocks and dive deep into the ocean, to follow the ship's trail from below.

Sweethaven For Sale

When I entered the ocean, I was prepared for thousands of units of empty sea. What I found instead was a thriving ecosystem filled with endless fish. Or, well, *thriving*—they weren't doing much and didn't seem too happy to be here. I vaguely remember a few fish from the very first level, but I hadn't seen a single one after that.

In fact, the schools of fish get in the way. They delay my swaps until Sweettooth's ship is out of reach.

"Out—of—my—way!"

The fish look at me with those dumb, bulging eyes.

"You're not supposed to be here," some of them hiss.

"Oh, hello, I am a *big chunky octopus*. The sea is the perfect place for me, thank you very much."

"The sea? You're not in the sea."

"Am I going insane or are you?"

Suddenly, a few fish evaporate. I didn't see them match—not even close. Yet their final sounds were cries of joy. I can understand their happiness due to getting away from *this weird place.*

"You're in Sweethaven," they say. "Or, well, all the way at the bottom of it. The part you want to be the least."

"You mean Bitterhell."

"If that's what you want to call it."

"Why does the game turn everyone into fish when they match outside of a level?"

"It's the … lowest form," the goldfish states solemnly.

I frown. "Spiders. Those are the lowest form. Fish are fine."

The fish around me shake their fins. "Some forms are more liked than others by humans. Players subconsciously use them more for matching. Like … how people connect more with a *pirate* than with a a *chocolate bar.*"

"Well I don't know about that. Seems to me chocolate would be at the top of the food chain."

"The developers didn't think so. They gave all the forms a *number*—their value or worth—and fish are zero."

Even more fish disappear, cheering. I point at them. "Where do they go?"

"Back into a level of course!"

I sigh, frustrated. "So your entire goal in life is to reach Sweethaven … only to get reincarnated as some other form the next time the Player plays!?"

The fish look at each other, unsure if this is a joke or not.

"Well, surely, isn't the greatest gift in life that you can keep playing?"

"I …"

I'm not sure. I guess?

Sweethaven starts to make sense now. On instinct, I swap toward the water surface, until I realize I don't have to anymore. My tentacles allow me to pull and push on existing items, giving me more freedom in movement.

Once I break through the surface, I am surrounded by *hundreds* of varying items. They are chilling, talking, *waiting* to be pulled back into a level and get a chance to play again. At the lowest level, right on the shore line, are the candies. The pirate items are slightly higher, though there's still a hierarchy between them. A treasure chest is a "higher form" than a barrel. And on top of all those items sit several pirates who look just like my previous form.

If you match, you end up here. If you match inside a level, you go *up* a form. Otherwise, you go *down* a form. But if you wait long enough, you will always be pulled out of Sweethaven to be part of a level again.

I can see how that is a comforting thought to these items. But …

"What happens if you're already the lowest form, a fish, and you go down again?"

"You die for real."

Okay, no, I take it back. I hate Sweethaven.

"And what is the highest form?"

Several items point to the island in the distance. Sweethaven is merely a location on the map where nothing happens and no level is placed. There isn't some border or gate separating it.

"What do you think? That highest form is so unreachable that only one entity ever made it."

"Sweettooth," I say, stunned. "He was used so often, won so many levels, played so well … that he became the highest form in the game. The only one to do it."

Surely he will see we are a perfect match … if I become literally like him? If I am able to go up one more form, from Kraken to another Sweettooth.

"Can you help me go up more forms? I think I have a few Data Doubloons left to pay you!"

They all shake their head, or twist their fins, or ruffle their feathers.

"We can't do anything," another pirate says. "As long as we're here."

Alright, I can't expect too much from this place. I'll have to do this myself.

I thank the entities in Sweethaven, at all levels, and continue my path to the new island. They're already playing level 7. That's why items are regularly pulled from here to get a new try at life in *Pirate Pound*.

As I draw closer, I don't notice any new elements. With delayed moves, and no interference from me, the Player struggles immensely with clearing the level.

Which is why they enlisted help.

Instead of *one* item lighting up—when their finger is touching it—there are often *two* items lighting up. One has a red glow, and one a blue. One selected item shows a profile picture of a cat, the other of a flamingo who jumps.

Ah, of course.

Squiggly lines and radio signals erupt from the entire level. As if all the items are calling someone on their phone, or a cartoon earthquake happens constantly.

The Player and their friend must have connected the devices somehow. They are close to each other, maybe in the same room, and trying to beat the level together. Sweettooth mostly stands by and watches, hoping, wishing.

I use my tentacles to drag myself onto the beach from the side. Sweettooth notices me, but doesn't react. I move straight at him, but get sidetracked when a part of the level *explodes* due to one of those items in a glass battle. Two Players playing means double the chaos.

The objective is to move 5 ships down *and* clear 50 treasure chests. They're going to reach it, unless they do something really stupid. Feelings of frustration and impatience still reach me, a straight connection between me and the Player. I understand now, especially since I added that 10 second delay to *every move*.

I notice this island has an identical layout to some of the previous levels. This allows me to find the Codeheart with ease, touch it, and undo my change.

Not only that, I completely *rip out* the hint system.

All this time, we've been preventing the Player from playing the game. We gave them no choice or thousands of choices that were all the same. We should just … let the game be the game, and let them play it. Even if that means losing once in a while or getting stuck due to dumb moves.

Because surely, as a wise fish told me just now, isn't the greatest gift to be able to keep playing?

When I return to the level, I freeze in my tracks. I can hear their *voices*. Soft, barely audible, but I can hear two kids yelling at each other as they try to play the game together. They *are* in the same room and their microphones are picking up this conversation.

I crawl closer and closer to hear their words. It's two young girls speaking in frantic, high-pitched voices.

"Your game really *is* waaaaay different from mine," one of them says.

"Hu-uh. It also keeps changing like every day."

Sweettooth interrupts the conversation with a loud roar. He waves his arms, a panicked look on his face.

"Where the hints be gone? We almost be losing, aye!"

When they see me, that anger is directed to my face.

"You be ruining the game once more, ain't you be Wildebyte?"

"Strange," I say, trying to stay calm. "I thought you of all entities would understand what it means to manipulate a game to your wishes."

The Player—or Players, I guess—barely make the objective and clear the level. As it dissolves, items happily jumping on the ship, Sweettooth stares me down.

"You think insulting me be the way to earrrrn friendship back?"

"Maybe you aren't *worth* my friendship."

The ship is ready to take off. The Player tugs on it by tapping the button to continue. But Sweettooth isn't ready to drop the subject.

"Thanks to you, I still don't be having a sword in my hand!" he roars. "You brought the game to the brink of uninstall. You made us weak so Bluetooth could swoop in and steal back their treasure! And you never even be making excuses!"

Wait—*steal back* their treasure?

A waterfall of realizations crashes over me, overwhelms me, brings out the worst anger that makes you feel sick in the stomach from your own rage.

My tentacles lash out and grab the ship. They are strong enough to crush the wood right then and there, I can feel it. Sweettooth takes a step back, mumbling *dark demon*, caressing his trusty ship as if that would save it.

"Coooould you maybe do this another time," Brad interrupts with that never-ending smile. "Ads are eager to be shown! Player wants to play!"

"No!" I yell. "I need to make a point to this *empty-skulled pirate!*"

GUILD WOULD NOT ALLOW IT

The ship sails away; I stay attached to it. My tentacles are eager to play the crushing animation. To stop any chance of Sweettooth getting his Toffee Treasure back. To destroy any chance of this game being played ever again.

He should pay for what he did to this game! He's an *idiot* for refusing my friendship! Why can't people give me a second chance!?

I roar. I flex my tentacles, embracing the ship. And I *crush*.

On open sea, halfway between level 7 and level 8, all the entities come to life. Swords cut into my tentacles. Barrels sacrifice themselves to save the ship's hull. Parrots peck at my tentacles to pry them loose.

I manage to break a part at the back before I am detached from the ship.

"Don't you see?" I yell at the items. "This was never Sweettooth's game. This is *Bluetooth's game!*"

Some of the items take my side. It's mostly fish and palm trees, but hey, I'll take what I can get.

We go in for the next attack.

"Aye, and Bluetooth made a mess of it," Sweettooth barks at me.

His sharp knives ward off my tentacle from the left, but are too late against the attack on the right. I snatch what remains of the mast and *rip* it off the ship. Items swap rapidly to form a rope of pirates holding hands to grab the mast.

"Sweettooth is the oppressor!" I look at him directly. "*You* are the enemy, Bluetooth is the real boss."

"And what did Bluetooth be doing, aye?"

Sweettooth directs the items still at his side, even though their number is shrinking. The swords form up to create one huge sword that *cuts* one of my tentacles. The pain is almost as bad as dying because we ran out of lives.

"Nothing!" the pirate roars. "He'd let the game die a slow death! The Player played *once* in two years before I took over."

"True pirate's words," I yell. "Kicking someone out of their home because they think they know better!"

Sweettooth is red-faced. "How easily you want others to give you a second chance, third chance, fourth chance. But give it to me? No no, the great Wildebyte would neverrrr!"

Enraged, my other tentacle swoops in and wraps around Sweettooth's frame, which now seems small and fragile in comparison. More usable items, such as pirates and swords, jump ship. They swap with each other to stay on my moving tentacles at all times, chipping away at the ship wherever possible.

The campaign ship is sinking.

Sweettooth floats in the air, held up only by one of my tentacles.

More and more items leave his side to join me. Perhaps because it is the only side without wet feet. Perhaps because they are smart enough to join the winning team.

Him and five swords make a last ditch attempt. They thrust their sharpest edges at my tentacle all at once. It is *cut* off again, throwing Sweettooth in freefall for just a few frames.

But another tentacle catches him as his feet touch the water, while a second tentacle swats the remaining items away. The move sends them flying into the air as if fired by a catapult.

Sweettooth drops his usual look that's half-grim and half-brave. He looks *frightened to death.*

"Mercy! Mercy!" he yells. "Where is your pirate's *honorrrr!?*"

I spit just past his face. I could eat him just like that. I could crush him.

The waves bring us to level 8 anyway. The ship is wrecked and floats in twenty pieces to all different corners of the pirate map.

The items hop onto the beach, eager to get away from whatever happens now. I am left on the shoreline with Sweettooth pleading for his life, dangling just a few units above a water block.

"I ... would *never* ... murder anybody," I hiss. "If you think I would do that, then you never really knew me at all."

I drop him in the sand.

I direct my voice to him, to all the items. "I was wrong to force you to follow my commands, just as I was wrong to take the game away from the Player. I admit that was a mistake and I try to be better."

I stick out one tentacle—that isn't wounded—to help Sweettooth get up.

"I have powers. Great powers that could destroy a game at any time. I try to use them well, but I can never be sure."

To that statement, all items can nod in agreement.

"Just because someone made a mistake, though," I say, "doesn't mean you *have* to stay angry or get revenge. It doesn't mean you can *never* be with them again."

Sweettooth looks incredulous. His eyes have trouble focusing, switching between my face and my tentacle, until he finally accepts the offer and lets me pull him to his feet.

"Aye," he says softly. "Because you not be agreeing with my methods, not be meaning they are wrong."

I swallow a nasty retort. His methods are … disagreeable. But so are mine, in the eyes of others. Sometimes. I guess. I mean, everyone else is usually wrong, right? I am nearly perfect, thank you very much.

"We should be able to Gamewalk together," I tell him. "Just because it's nice to play. Nice to have each other. Not because of what we can or can't give each other, not because we 100% agree on everything."

I glare at Brad, who waits impatiently until he can show another ad.

"Gamewalking together would not be a contract," I say, "or a deal, or something you pay for. We *should* be able to just play together and that's that."

Sweettooth looks skeptical. "There arrrr limits, Wildebyte. Did you never consider I was forced to do everything I did? That the code be making me do it? The Guild programmed me this way and I *can't stop it*, no matter how much I would like. The Guild would never allow me to Gamewalk with you! They wouldn't allow it, aye!"

He dusts off his uniform and prepares himself to play the level. "Some things just be wrong. And some people just be incompatible."

"And some people just lie to themselves," I say. My strength leaves me; my tentacles sag and my eyelids droop. "Not giving anything a proper chance."

"I gave you a chance, didn't I?" he says. "I never attacked you, did I? *You* attacked me first."

"And … and … some people listen too much to made-up rules by some Guild that never shows its face. This is the wild west! Handheld Ludra has no actual rules!"

"In here, confusing demon, I must follow my code," he says. "That's why I Gamewalk. Being inside another game is the *only* moment I can be free. And I can't do that unless we steal back my Toffee Treasure."

"I promise I'll protect everyone. I'll make it possible to follow the rules and still be free."

"No, no, no," Sweettooth says with a shake of his head. "No, no—"

"We can do *anything* if we just try."

"No, maybe *you* can. *We* can't."

He gives me a slanted grin, then turns away. His voice never sounded so rough and frail.

"People don't think it be that way, but it do."

With that, he seems to have lost his fear for me, and I am lost completely as to what to do.

The Player starts the level, and so Sweettooth must play. We stand beside each other in silence, just hoping the Player does the right moves and doesn't waste more of our time.

A few levels ago we stumbled upon a black, unusable square after creating a 2 by 2 pattern. Back then, we were too early. Now it is finally unlocked.

When the two Players create that pattern, a Kraken appears. Much smaller and more square than me, but still recognizable.

And when you swap the Kraken with any other item, *all* instances of that item are removed immediately. It allows them to reach some very tough spots and rake in points quickly. In fact, before the game is over, they've made it their goal to create as many Krakens as possible. They also talk about it in the real-life conversation, which is more audible now that my tentacles are pressed against the level.

This tactic is seemingly brilliant, because they clear the level in one go.

As level 9 is highlighted and unlocked on the treasure map, everyone looks at me.

"Oh wise Wildebyte," Sweettooth says while pretending to pray to me, "how do you propose we now be moving to the next island, aye? Or your master plan be to remove all ships and then figure it out later?"

"I was hoping *you* could provide the master plans," I say. "You've shown yourself capable of pretty deep schemes. Tell me, will Bluetooth put up a fight? How easy will it be to get back both our treasures? Can't we just *skip* level 9?"

I can't wait to get my hands on my Lost Memory. I've been racking my brain trying to remember what it looked like when Bluetooth stole it, but it was just too far to see. Might it give me a clue about where my parents are?

"Skip? *Skip?*" several items say. "What heresy!"

"Nah, heresy be my middle name," Sweettooth says with a grin. "But we're forced to play levels in order."

He and all the items climb on top of me. Great. They've decided that I will be their vehicle of choice.

"He'll put up a fight, alright. One of us will not make it out alive, I be sure of that. So let's play a little longer, shall we?"

In a softer voice, he adds. "Also, the Guild would not allow it."

Prepare To Plunder

I was right about Sweettooth being the planner. He has scammed his game into believing *he* was the master and Bluetooth the enemy for *years*. Preparing a surprise attack on Bluetooth's island was like making a grocery list to him.

"Alright, so we be entering the island at night, dark-cloaked and stealthy. I *believe* playing—and winning—level 10 will open the Unmatchable Underworld to us. Both our treasures will be hidden somewhere inside there. We be going in, we be grabbing what's ours, and we be leaving before dawn."

"Sounds like a plan," I say. "And what if Bluetooth does notice us? What if winning level 10 isn't opening any magical gates?"

"Aye, but for improvisation we have *you*." He grins before walking away again. Always busy, that man. "If you let yourself be."

His comments gnaw at my brain, though. He truly believes that I am too … nice? Whereas other entities called me a troublemaker and lawbreaker, he seems annoyed that I actually follow rules and try to play nice. He expected me to turn into a dragon at will and transform games into other games at the touch of my finger—while in reality, I play along as if I'm just an entity, just as much in the dark as the others.

Even if I wanted to change that … I wouldn't know how.

As I bring everyone across the sea, I get a good overview of the path we already walked. It feels so long ago that I entered this game. That island that was completely covered in ice? Yeah, it isn't anymore. The part that turned out to be Sweethaven? Covered in mist now, probably unfindable to anyone who isn't a lost Kraken.

As the Level Ship drops the items for level 9, I see all the special items we've learned along the way, and the special objectives. This one is about removing all those *cursed* locations. This playing field is also far bigger than the previous levels, including a new type of edge. It only appears at the top or bottom of items, never to the sides.

As usual, it only reveals its purpose through *playing* the game.

My modifications basically made it impossible for us to influence it any more. We can't give any more hints nor play the game for them. The real Players are having fun, but that doesn't necessarily mean they're doing the best moves.

In fact, quite the opposite. I hear them laughing their ass off as they set a new challenge: both of them may only do swaps with one of three types. This obviously causes them to lose level 9, but they don't care, because they have infinite lives now.

They retry with a new challenge. One of them may only do horizontal swaps, the other only vertical swaps.

That's actually an interesting challenge to give yourself. Both Sweettooth and I stand next to the level trying to solve the puzzle as well, following their made-up rules. And we both do it with a smile.

"Okay, I'll pretend to be the jumpy flamingo," I say. "I guess I would do *that* move."

"I be the one whose dad is certainly not the president," Sweettooth says with a laugh. "My move would swap those ships, gives two explosions."

I nod in approval. Then the Players take their turn and we see what the new edges do: they *teleport*. Items that fall down into such an edge, reappear from another edge. As if the two ends were connected with an invisible tunnel.

That makes the level considerably harder, as it's tough to predict where things will end up. The Players fail once more, but they still don't care. They're having fun and give it another try.

Halfway through, we can already see this going downhill.

"Arrr! An empty-skulled move by the not-president-dad!" Sweettooth swaps places with me. "Aye, let me be the flamingo person. They're much smarter."

"Yeah, because *I* helped them," I say jokingly. A few frames later, they do the dumbest move imaginable, which only removes three treasure chests at the top row and does nothing else.

"See, now that I'm gone—"

"Oh shut your beak."

The Players try and try again, as long as it stays fun. And we're there to play along and watch with pleasure. Just playing the game. Just playing the game for a little moment, without some looming threat or burning haste. Just trying to beat these challenges together, side by side.

Surely, that is the greatest gift.

Brad agrees. The many failures give him ample opportunity to show some ads. Not because the Players get something for it—simply because the time restriction has passed and he can show an unprovoked ad again. I can hear the Players just walking away, going to the toilet, snacking some food, without ever really watching the ad.

*Tired of matching pirate and candy items all day?
Then this is your lucky day! Try our newest game: Catapult
Cats. Slingshot your way to victory and defeat the evil Space
Dogs! Download for free at—*

I sigh. Another ad that basically discourages the
Player to play the game and do something else
instead. Aren't game developers learning the lessons
I'm learning? Or do they just not care with how much
money they make?

Fortunately, now Pirate Pound is interesting
enough that the Players stay and try again.

Brad doesn't care that his ad isn't viewed at all.
As long as he's paid, I guess.

I don't know how long we stayed on this island,
retrying level 9 until it was burned inside the Players'
brains. They made one serious attempt, using all their
knowledge so far, and finally beat it.

All I know is that I had fun all the same.
Sweettooth and I tried to play along. Seeing the
Players figure it out and be happy … made us happy.
Much happier than inserting ourselves into the game
and *forcing* it.

As night falls, we go over the plan once more.
Sweettooth holds a torch, standing in the middle of
the beach. He addresses all his items.

"Tonight we claim victory, aye!" he says with
conviction. "We slay the beast!"

"Erm," I interrupt, "what he means is that we leave Bluetooth in one piece and just—"

"We take what's ours!"

"Yes, that and *nothing else*."

"And leave no palm tree left standing! No stone unturned! No ship unwrecked!"

"We will," I interrupt, "leave everything intact and Bluetooth sleeping."

Sweettooth drops his head in his hands. "Wildebyte, if we to be Gamewalking together, we really need to work on not interrupting each other's speeches."

Am I imagining things or does he seem more open to the idea now? No, no, don't get my hopes up. This has happened like five times now. And every time there's a new reason we just don't work together. I can't sing. His hair stinks. I can barely understand half his sentences.

"Let's *destroy* our enemies! No mercy from the black skulls!"

Raising his torch, shouting, Sweettooth looks more menacing than ever. The items quickly join him with cheers and roars. Perhaps they just want him to get his treasure back, so he can Gamewalk and *leave them alone* most of the time.

Looking at Sweettooth's intimidating silhouette, and how easily he still sways the scared items to his side, puts the final nail in the coffin for me.

Sweettooth does not break stuff by accident, does not ruin games to reach some higher goal, does not steal money to give to the poor. They are a *pirate*. A cowboy in the wild west who would ditch me the moment they get bored of me. Could I really work and travel together with someone like that?

He is right. I'm being way too nice and sticking to the rules, while he would like to do whatever he pleases. He probably hasn't even *considered* the consequences of his Gamewalking or killing Bluetooth.

We're different, alright. We are no match.

Is that really a problem, though?

Or does it just mean we actually complement each other?

As everyone prepares to leave, I seek out Brad.

"Researchers still there with you?" I ask.

"No," he says. "Once you declined them, they invested resources elsewhere."

I nod. "You, erm, have known Sweettooth longer than me. Does he mean it? Will there be … death and plundering on this mission?"

Brad looks at me and drops his smile. "I won't say there won't be."

"What?"

"You will not hear me saying that he will not not refrain from doing a full-on attack with blatant disregard for everything."

Brad sees my confused face and looks apologetic. "Sorry, marketing talk."

I sigh. "I'll just have to rein him in, don't I?"

"They're a pirate, Wildebyte," Brad says as he already climbs on one of my tentacles. "What did you expect? They steal stuff from other games and plunder the device. They break the rules not because they hate them specifically, but because they're against rules and responsibility in the first place. They have never been a real person, so why would they have the morals of a real person?"

I wait in silence until all the items, which includes Sweettooth, are on my back and tentacles. I instinctively move to island 10 by *swapping*, until I realize I want to test Sweettooth's comments. Can I just … not follow the rules? Could I somehow just move normally?

I don't get a chance to test it, because Sweettooth stands on my head and roars: "Prepare to Plunderrrrrr!"

So much for our stealthy approach.

BLUETOOTH'S ISLAND

Shockingly, nobody woke up from Sweettooth's roar. At least, not that we can see or hear. I am able to climb onto a silent and dark beach. No torch or item in sight. I can't even see well enough to know what's beyond the next few sandy hills.

Nobody wants to be the first to properly enter the island. The items point at everything they see and whisper to each other, but nobody makes a move.

Sweettooth steels himself and is the first to jump into the sand. He purposely kicks some of it in my eyes with a satisfied grin. I blow through my nose to completely *cover* him in sand.

"What?" I whisper. "It's a *great* camouflage disguise."

"Cooooould I interest you in a fan or a hair dryer? Buy one now for—"

"I be fine."

As we sneak towards the heart of the island, I must say I'm disappointed. It's exactly the same as the previous few islands! Everything is the same size, at the same location. The only differences are superficial, such as Bluetooth's ship docked at

167

harbor, or the entrance to his Underworld leaning against the Codeheart area.

In that same area, the level is supposed to be played. A wooden sign notifies us that we're entering *Level 10* at *our own peril* and *cowards be turning back now.* It pushes a brief wave of hesitation through the group, until everyone shrugs and continues.

"We must be being quick," Sweettooth whispers. "We must start level 10 ourselves, without the Player, and clear it. Preferably in one try."

How do we do that, though? Sweettooth looks at me.

"If you told me this earlier," I whisper, "I could've already thought about how to do it!"

"Nah, as I be saying, you're better when improvising."

I touch the sign and look at its code, but it has no trigger to start the level. I walk around the area, tentacles caressing every single object, trying to find something to start level 10.

"I don't know!" I whisper, exasperated. "Nothing is connected to the level itself here."

The items grow restless. The jungle around us buzzes with the noise of insects and … less explainable noises. Clicks. Stomps. Grunts. Sound effects with no clear origin.

They shift around, constantly looking over their shoulder, but nobody has noticed us so far.

Still, they decide to light *one* torch to push away the darkness.

It is helpful, yes. Because now I can finally see that there is a literal *ship's rudder* bolted to a stone, and rotating it starts the level.

It is also our downfall, because now we can see at least ten enemies sleeping nearby. The sight sends many items shivering. I freeze, moving less freely than before.

"We just be extra quiet and careful," Sweettooth says to calm them down.

As the level starts, the items are placed into neat stacks one by one. We bypassed the Level Ship, we bypassed the need for a Player, so now we have to play ourselves.

All of this goes well, until the *sound effects* start coming in. Random happy noises to get the Player excited to start. Random even happier noises whenever you perform a successful match.

"Turn it off! Turn it off!" Sweettooth hisses.

"I'm trying!"

Two enemy pirates have woken up. Groggily they wander towards Sweettooth. He doesn't hesitate and punches them both unconscious in one swing.

"Stop gawking at me with those black-marbled eyes! Be fixing it, aye!"

I travel around the area. Palm trees bend and almost break as I climb into them to see what they hide. That's how I find two small *speakers* around the area creating all this noise.

Following Sweettooth's example, I give them a good punch to destroy them. And also to hurt my own tentacles more than I would like. As they fall to pieces, the volume and pitch of their sound effects drops and drops until it vanishes.

The torch is put out. The faint glow of the items is enough to work with. In silence and dim light, Sweettooth and I try to find our best move.

"If we start there," Sweettooth says, "we'll get an item in a glass bottle for later."

"Yeah," I say, stroking my chin with a tentacle. "But it doesn't help us remove those ice blockers, which we should do first, no?"

"Maybe," he says.

"This is hard. Level 10 is hard. I don't know, just, just you do something. We don't have time to think."

Sweettooth grins. "We do my plan, obviously."

He climbs into the level to perform that swap. It's a fine choice.

We pick up the pace, alternating who gets the final decision on what to do. There are some great moves, there are some mediocre moves, and in the end … we fail.

No sound effect, of course. Also no glitters and confetti, because we failed. Though I *do* need to turn that off as well to prevent more—

Several more enemies wake up. Sweettooth is distracted fighting them. More and more, he is drawn into the jungle, using nothing but his knives and bare fists to knock out the other pirates.

I have to retry the level alone. Making decisions is *hard*. I can see all the swaps, all the moves, their good and their bad, and then I just *freeze*. Unable to pick any one of them.

I hadn't realized how much of our previous success was thanks to Sweettooth. Thanks to his way of just being confident and deciding to do *something*.

I try to adopt the same line of thinking. Just pick an option, quickly. That's better and more fun than thinking for hours to find the perfect move.

I close my eyes and start climbing the level blind. Wherever I end up, *that's* what I do.

"Are you empty-skulled!?" Sweettooth yells from behind the level. I hear a hit, a grunt, a body falling against a palm tree. "Open your eyes!"

"It's fine," I say. I end up next to a treasure chest that was a good move anyway. I execute the swap before I can hesitate.

I keep telling myself to adopt the pirate mindset. And it works. It helps make the decisions faster and play the level faster.

I still *fail*.

But this time I failed within a minute, instead of ten minutes.

So I can try again more quickly. And on this third attempt, the stars—or items, I guess—seem to align. Everything falls in the right place for some big explosions and special items early on. I get lucky with the placement of some ice blocks, removing them all with the first move.

This is it. I want to tell Sweettooth, but he's busy fighting the last of the enemy fighters, and I don't want to be distracted.

The next time I remind myself to think like Sweettooth, my form changes. My tentacles disappear. They shrink, shrivel, like a plant growing but played in reverse, until they're just *arms*. My huge head with monstrous teeth becomes a regular human head, and only one of its teeth turns gold.

I have become Sweettooth too.

I see the final few moves. I also see the sun rising. I pick one option that will probably get us close to the goal, and another, and then finally—

Some flying object *crashes* through the level.

The items explode in every direction. The level immediately recognizes something is wrong and fails itself—silently. Sweettooth darts back to the area to help me out with this new enemy.

"You … be me?" he says, shock on his face.

"I … be you?"

The level immediately repairs itself and is ready to go again.

"Ah! Good job!" he says triumphantly.

"I'm not doing that!" I must admit.

Instead, the Players have come back to play. Together. Which also means the Camera follows and anything in its view must now adhere to their code again.

We look around to find who or what killed my *perfect, genius attempt* at clearing level 10.

A pirate stands on the beach, dusting off sand. He's as tall as both of us, so not a regular pirate item. His appearance is entirely *blue* and radio waves are emitted from all over his body.

Instead of a wooden leg, he has a … broken vacuum cleaner?

"Ah, aye see you still have my present from last time," Sweettooth says with a grin.

I frown. "From what game could you possibly have stolen a *broken vacuum cleaner*?"

When Bluetooth turns it on in reverse, it acts like a *jetpack* that shoots him into the sky.

"You be annoying me one last time, Sweettooth—and no, bringing two of you will not be saving you from *death and destruction*, aye!" he bellows.

I nudge Sweettooth. "Hey, he talks the same way as you do!"

"That be the *only* thing we have in common."

"Well, no, you're also both pirates, and—"

"Cooooould I interest you in a *sword* to fight off this evil pirate with bad dental care?" Brad interjects.

"Well yes, why didn't you—"

"ATTACK!" Bluetooth roars. The echoes of his voice shake palm trees across the entire island and make the stones shiver.

This conversation revealed to Bluetooth who is the *real* Sweettooth. They charge so quickly that Sweettooth stumbles backward, unable to defend himself after losing his knives and being exhausted from fighting.

So I jump in front of him.

I'm plucked from the beach, taken into the sky, then dropped *hard* against a large rock formation.

I discover a new experience in Ludra. I pass out.

IMPOSSIBLE CHOICE

When I come to my senses, I immediately hear the dull thuds and explosions of fighting going on elsewhere. Once in a while, the floor shakes, which means I shake with it. I wasn't out for long, but every frame counts now.

Bluetooth looms over me.

"Who are you and why would you *ever* be sacrificing yourself for that scumbag?"

I smile. "I'm Sweettooth, can't you see?"

"You not be. You be an imposter." Bluetooth circles me like a shark. "I be asking around. I be keeping an eye out on developments in this game and Ludra. And they be talking about a dark demon who used to be a *real* human … does that be ringing a bell?"

"My ears are ringing, alright," I say, trying to shake off my blurry vision and prickling ears.

"Aye. They also said the demon makes bad jokes all the time."

Bluetooth grabs my collar and roughly pulls me off the floor. We stare in each other's eyes for a moment, as he reaches for the sword on his side. In a flash, he is ready to cut my head off.

Instinctively, without thinking, I reach into the ropes that tied me up. I mess with the code, free myself, then turn the rope into a lasso.

I catch the sword and rip it from their hand.

Then I try to catch *him*, but Bluetooth is fast enough to step back. He readies a new sword, its sharp tip pointed at my heart.

He licks his lips. The blueness of his face makes it seem as if he's always cold and out of breath, but I can already tell he's the most capable fighter I've met so far.

"This will not be ending well," he says after a long silence. "Whoever wins this fight, the game will suffer. *They* will suffer."

He puts away his sword. Finally at ease, I can check out my surroundings. My back was against a large rock, identical to one that was in the center of all the other identical islands. We're deep inside the jungle and a good hundred units from where they are playing level 10. Unfortunately, having turned off all sound, I can't hear if they are doing well.

"You know I am too strong," Bluetooth says. "You probably also know by now that this is *my* game, not Sweettooth's."

"And now you know that I am too strong," I say.

"So, as I be saying, this fight will merely destroy everything until only one remains. Do you want that …

Wildebyte?"

"Of course not."

"Then I be offering you a choice."

Bluetooth points at the lines radiating from his entire body. "You know why two players can connect devices? You know why they can play together now? Because of *me*. I make a technology possible called Bluetooth."

"A bit weird to name it after yourself, but okay."

"This device is connected to a different phone. We're constantly using radio signals to send information to each other, such as which swap we want to do and what the level looks like now. All of that goes through *me*. All of that is possible thanks to *me*."

They come closer and closer. I notice they still need to *swap* with items while on the ground; if they want actual free movement, they need to use their vacuum-cleaner-jetpack-mechanism.

"I heard the Wildebyte doesn't like it here—and we don't like the Wildebyte. Surely ... you would like to be transferred to a *different* device?"

I was prepared to turn down any offer from this blue guy.

But this one stings.

Jumping to a different device? Where I could get a fresh start? With my knowledge so far, I might be able to hide my Outsider status and get all entities to love me. Perhaps this device was just a failed attempt and my real adventures start in that other device.

Or maybe I should stop running away the moment things don't work out perfectly, exactly as I wanted. Maybe the only way to grow is to actually learn from the failure instead of fleeing from it.

Bluetooth already takes my silence for agreement. He smiles and comes even closer, preparing to touch me and send me away. He knows this is an impossible choice, a dilemma so hard for me that it might as well not be a choice at all.

Which makes it both scary and satisfying to utter the following word.

"No."

He freezes. "No? Did you not hear the offer? A fresh start in a new, not broken device!"

"I'd rather keep playing the game than flee because I didn't win last time."

"What ... but ... "

He's distracted. I assemble all my power and attack.

I manage to hit him hard in the stomach and the face. He responds by grabbing me and taking to the skies again.

It gives me a nice overview of the whole island. No, he takes us even higher. I get a view of the entire path we traveled so far. Something bugs me. Some thought nagging at me, but I can't make it make sense.

Especially not with a flying blue pirate trying to smash my face. Or should I say *pound* my—

Ouch!

I grapple with him in the air. Once I wriggle myself free, I kick at this leg until it stops pushing us further upward.

"You broke my leg!"

We start our downward arc. But at this height? I should still have plenty of time to find a safe landing.

The real Players are trying level 10. Sweettooth is fighting for his life, overwhelmed by hordes of enemy pirates. The items can't help him out as they are forced to stay within the level.

The suspense kills me. The lack of control feels wrong too, as now the outcome of the entire battle is in the hands of two silly, ignorant teenagers. All I feel is their *fun*. All I hear is their vivid conversation about the battles happening around the level and how realistic and awesome it all feels.

The Players have only a few moves left. They won't make it, not this time.

I avert my eyes. On every shoreline, all around the island, fights have broken out. I thought it would be just Bluetooth and a few guards, maybe a few ships.

But Bluetooth has proven himself to be the original boss of the game. The number of soldiers he is able to field, the number of ships and cannons creating holes in the island, is overwhelming.

Sweettooth is forced back. He has lost both his knives and stumbles backward into the level area, just before a broken palm tree falls on him.

The Players fail level 10.

The hardest part isn't staying alive. The hardest part is keeping the enemies away so that the Players can keep playing the level.

It resets. They try again.

Bluetooth aims for the soft landing of some palm trees. I try to kick him away, but he keeps a hold of me, using me to *steer*.

I reach for his sword. He grabs it himself and aims at me, as we tumble through the sky at a speed that makes me fear we'll *ignite* any moment now. Instinctively, I sent a *blast* of power into his arm. It dislodges the sword—but Bluetooth is fast and nimble enough to catch it with his other hand.

We're racing towards the palm trees now.

Sweettooth enters my peripheral vision. Exhausted, leaning against a palm tree, he screams at Brad, who is cheery and calm as always. Probably can't be killed. Lucky boy.

Two enemies approach Sweettooth from the back.

"Watch out!" I yell, but Bluetooth puts a hand on my mouth. We're too far away anyway.

Then Sweettooth produces a *huge* pile of shining Data Doubloons. He hands them to Brad with a disgusted, almost teary look on his face. Brad accepts them with repeated thanks and then produces a new *sword*.

Sweettooth grabs it and immediately strikes down the two enemies attacking from behind, as if he had eyes in his back.

The Players are doing … great? They're racking up points and already cleared two of the three objectives. They just need a few not-terrible moves and its game over.

Bluetooth and I *crash* into a palm tree, which bounces us to another palm tree, which then bounces us back into the sandy beach area.

We're forced to let go and land far away from each other. Bluetooth is enraged, his face turning more *purple* than *blue*. He foams at the mouth, raising his sword again.

Items swap in and out of view. Enemy or friend, I can't tell anymore. Both must use the other elements of this island to even move around, which means rocks and barrels enter my view, only to be displaced a frame later. Fishes and parrots float through my view by swapping with treasure chests and palm trees, turning the island inside-out over time.

The enemy shoots cannon balls that explode when matched, three or more in a row. We displace them before it happens, so they explode at a safe distance, or so early that the enemies send *themselves* to the opposite of Sweethaven.

Until a wave of sand forces me to the floor again. I look up.

The Players made it! Level 10 is cleared! That social connection—playing together—really did a lot for this game, huh?

The entrance to the cave opens quickly, sending a rumbling earthquake through the entire island. From my perspective, the inside is complete darkness, with two very faint stars in the distance.

Sweettooth gives me a thumbs up. Yeah, sure, that will help when fighting Bluetooth.

"Prepare to Plunderrrr!" he yells as he races into the cave to rescue his Toffee Treasure and my Lost Memory.

You Need Imagination

Enemies enter the cave after him, trying to crowd the entrance and make sure Sweettooth never gets out. I have to stand by and watch it happen. Bluetooth takes all my attention. He attacks ferociously, scoring cuts and bruises all over my body. He exposes my complete lack of experience fighting any competent enemy.

Please get out. Please get out with *both* our treasures.

Then I remember. Sweettooth *with* his sword is unstoppable.

One by one, the enemies at the cave entrance are kicked aside or forced to swap until they are *stuck* in the cave walls. A sword flashes and dances. It leaves white trails cutting through item after item, creating a hole out of which the pirate can crawl.

Sweettooth appears carrying a treasure chest and a purple glowing … what's that?

It's a statue. Its materials a blend of rock, gold, and wood. A statue of my parents, side by side, holding me as a baby. They are dressed like explorers. Mother seems … mad at me? But Father smiles at me.

It almost appears to me like the statue of holy figures, like a capture of some historical event.

"Give it to me! Throw it!" I yell to Sweettooth.

"I would, but—"

Carrying the treasures made it near impossible to also carry the sword. He has to drop both to defend himself.

Ignoring Bluetooth charging at my back, I swap my way to my own Lost Memory. It rolls through the sand and comes to a stop against the *Level 10* sign.

Too slow! Too—I send blast after blast of energy to overwrite the swapping code with all I have.

And it just … steps aside for me. As if the code understands that it's better to let me do my thing than to stand in my way. I can walk and run now. I am free from that core rule of the game.

And so I run until my legs buckle under me, almost touching my Lost Memory, before Bluetooth dashes past me and kicks it aside.

"I *hate* blue pirates!"

"Aye! On that we agree!" Sweettooth says.

He cuts down a few enemies, but misses the final one carrying his Toffee Treasure. The enemy pirate quickly dances away, swapping with palm trees and using them as a shield. Sweettooth has to find another way around.

I chase Bluetooth deeper into the jungle. I'm wasting time here. Even if we get these things, he won't just let us leave. We need to actually *win* this—

That's what my mind was trying to tell me.

These past few islands were identical. And they are *almost* in a straight line.

I stop the chase, to Bluetooth's surprise. Sweettooth is struggling to stay alive, far removed from his treasure. The enemy pirate grins, holding the treasure high above her head. She approaches a new part of the island that contains *many* similarly looking chests.

Sweettooth and I lock gazes. She *can't* be allowed to place the Toffee Treasure there; it would match three-in-a-row and disappear to Sweethaven.

I abandon my own Lost Memory. I make a run and leap for the enemy, who didn't expect me to move so freely. They rotate away, shielding the treasure, but are too slow. I kick it out of their hands, back to Sweettooth.

He smiles and nods gratefully, as he cradles the Toffee Treasure and prepares to bring it to safety.

"Get everyone off the island!" I tell him. "But do it, like, subtly. The enemies must not follow."

"What you be planning to do?" he says. "You don't need help? Here, take my sword."

"Nah, all I need is *imagination*."

Bluetooth taunts me with the Lost Memory. "I have it! Come chase me! Come fight me, coward!"

Sweettooth doesn't question my plan any further. He commands all the items to slowly retreat to the beach and then into the water.

I do the same thing, but at a different side of the island. This one is out of line with level 9 and level 8. If I can just *move* it ...

I jump into the water. On one side, I *remove* water blocks, leaving a nice gap. On the other side, I add more and more water, creating a forceful push against the island. I keep going back and forth, no matter how much Bluetooth taunts me, no matter how much I *want* my Lost Memory, because this is going to work.

It has to work.

Finally, the gap at the back is exactly large enough to bring the island in line. The force on the other side is so strong that—

The island rumbles. Cracks appear like veins running from the Codeheart.

And the *entire island* moves, slowly and hesitantly, into my gap.

Understanding flashes across the faces of both Bluetooth and Sweettooth.

"Stop it now!" Bluetooth yells. "Or I be destroying your Lost Memory!"

Our items are almost entirely off the island now. The enemy scrambles to do the same, but it's way too late.

The three islands—level 10, level 9, and level 8— form a straight line. And being identical islands, they match.

Three in a row.

"NOOOO!"

Bluetooth uses his sword to crush, slice and destroy my Lost Memory. It be useless now, Sweettooth might say. It be okay, I would answer.

All three islands *puff out of existence*.

The gigantic holes left behind are quickly filled with water blocks. All supporters of Bluetooth disappear with it, probably overcrowding Sweethaven now. Sweettooth and most of our items are safely in the water, standing on barrels or high palm trees.

Only Bluetooth remains. He crashes into the water and swims for his life.

Sweettooth starts the chase. Using a few barrels as a boat, and a palm tree as paddles, he is on Bluetooth in a matter of frames.

"Your days be over!" he yells. "Your incapable empty-skulled rein be coming to an end! This is revenge for trying to hurt my friend!"

He drops everything to grab his sword, aiming for Bluetooth.

"No!" I swim as fast as I can.

Sweettooth doesn't listen. His sword becomes a blur and leaves a white trail.

"*He* is responsible for connecting devices!" I yell. "Thanks to him the Player is playing again!"

He freezes mid-swing. Bluetooth nods aggressively to support my statement.

"Killing him would kill the game!"

I finally reach them and position myself between Sweettooth and Bluetooth.

"You hate each other, fine. But you still need each other to keep playing the game."

Sweettooth grips the handle of his sword even more tightly. His breathing is ragged, his eyes filled with anger.

"If two phones from different brands can be paired ... if the child of a president and some wacky classmate can be paired ... then why can't you two? Why can't we?"

Sweettooth spits past me and blows hot breath in my face. His sword is inches from Bluetooth's neck, as his arm shakes from the exhaustion of keeping the heavy weapon there.

Then he sheathes his sword.

"Because you be saving my life," he mumbles. "And my Toffee Treasure. Not because I agree."

My form reverts *back* to being a kraken, then a smaller pirate.

"That's ... fine?"

All the silly reasons we invented the past few weeks for why we couldn't work together are just that. Silly.

I nudge Sweettooth until he calms down and smiles at me. "You called me a friend! You called me a friend!"

"Aye, don't be making me regret it."

A new sword suddenly appears on his flotsam, bobbing in the calm waves as the sun rises. A purple sword with a purple glow.

A second Lost Memory?

I touch it before anyone else can. But no memory plays. I just ...

The events of the past hour replay before my eyes, right until the moment Sweettooth listens to me and spares Bluetooth.

This isn't a Lost Memory.

It's a New Memory.

I push it to my chest and cradle it, basking in its warmth, then put it away very carefully in a very safe location.

Sweettooth sticks out his hand. Bluetooth grabs it and is heaved onto the makeshift barrel boat. The two refuse to look at each other, but there just isn't enough space to *not* look at each other.

"I'm afraid I need you anyway," Sweettooth grumbles. "With my Toffee Treasure back, I be Gamewalking the rest of the year. So *you* can run this little game."

"That be my original job. It be fine."

"What happens if your home game is uninstalled while you're somewhere else?" I ask him.

"I be unsure. That be the scary part."

Sweettooth's actions in taking such tight control of the game make perfect sense to me now. Fearing his home game would die when he was away, ending him instantly. I probably would've done the same, especially when my experience with other games was still limited. It *is* still limited.

But I feel like that be changing soon.

Swapping with each other—some underwater, some above water—we move to the nearest plot of land left.

Sweettooth grins as he explains the secret behind the game exit to me. I could have figured it out sooner, I guess.

He opens his Toffee Treasure. He takes three gold coins from inside and places them in a row. At that exact location, a portal opens that leads into a game tunnel.

The pirate is eager to step in. I can't believe it. The game is in shambles! We need to clean up!

I hold him back. "We need to establish some rules."

OR NOT TO GAMEWALK

Sweettooth and I implement improvements for the game in an uncomfortable silence. He shoots me nervous glances and I don't know what they mean. Bluetooth does most of the talking.

"We should bring back the lives system, aye," he says. "It helps stop the player before they be too frustrated or bored."

"For some people, I guess," I say. "But let's make it optional. And you only lose a life if you *fail*."

Bluetooth nods. I keep a list of all the changes I need to make, the exact words or numbers that need modification, once I get to the Codeheart.

Brad walks close by, never really entering the conversation. I speak loudly: "But then we should also stop showing ads so people can gain more lives."

"Whaaaat?"

Brad jumps in and lists all the reasons why advertisements are the best thing to ever happen to society. His top reason is the fact that they pay for games like these to be free. All the reasons after that are lofty—and bad—arguments about creativity, freedom of speech, and even ads leading to world peace.

"Oh, and the Player often be losing by just one or two moves," Bluetooth says. "Seen it a thousand times in my time."

"Then we add some opportunity to overcome that."

"By displaying an *ad!*"

"No, Brad, by rewarding the players for Playing by giving them boosters like *five extra turns* or *remove five items of choice* if they reach high scores."

Sweettooth moves with the group, but still hasn't spoken. I just can't *read* his mysterious face.

"You know what we should really do?" I say, smiling. "Add random *challenges* to levels! Like those kids did on their own. Every time you play a level, you see a new optional challenge. Like *only perform swaps with red items* or *never use a treasure chest.*"

"Aye! That be more like it!" Bluetooth's eyes glaze over, as if he can already see the game it will become. "You … you can really make those changes?"

"I think so. Probably. Yes. If not on the first try, then I'll keep messing with code until—" That doesn't sound too confident. "I mean, yes, I know what I'm doing, thank you very much."

"Oh, and then maybe we be giving out special medals if somebody beats a level on their *first attempt.*

Aye? Aye?"

Bluetooth is completely ready to be the sole boss of this game once more.

I'm about to compliment him and say it's a great idea, until I realize it's not. This punishes the Player for playing the game again. Once they failed their first attempt, they can only get *fewer rewards* on the next attempts. And I'm sure Brad would abuse the system immediately to display ads in return for "pretending this is your first time."

"No," I say, "we can do better. We must reward the Player for playing. We must give them actual choice. So how about special medals when they clear the level in a good *time*? Or with a *really high* score? Something that entices them to keep playing, something they can try over and over?"

Bluetooth and Sweettooth both ponder this for a while. I am not quite sure I can even create such a complex system, but at least I can try.

I rack my brain for any other improvements. I only find one more. "Both us and the Players just really liked creating those special items. You know, the ones that give explosions. Let's just … do more of that? Higher chance and bigger explosions? More confetti? Let's just … follow that fun."

Bluetooth, Sweettooth and the items come up with a few more additions. Even more special rules, and patterns, and items, and mini-games, and types of islands. But I shut those down too. If I learned anything from the previous games, it's that a good game must stay *simple* and *streamlined*. If we add so many rules that players can't remember them all, they stop being able to actually play the game, and we've ruined it all.

After a short swapping journey, reach the Codeheart.

I go to work on the code. The word *Guild* is written all over it, but there's no explanation in sight. All I know is that they steal—or "get inspired by"—existing games. They saw *Sugar Stomp* and made *Pirate Pound*, a weird half-baked mix of elements stolen from that. They call it "cloning" themselves.

Sweettooth still stands behind me. He whistles a sea shanty.

Once I'm done carefully making changes and look up, he decides it's time.

"You just can't help following the rules, aye? Being a brave little Outsider. Manipulate as little as possible."

"It saved your life. It kept me alive. The code is written to be followed, I have learned."

He grips his sword until his knuckles turn white. "You say it like it be impressing me. Like some achivement. But it be a disappointment."

"You're disappointed I saved your life!?"

Sweettooth struggles to find the words. I guess I've found the limits of their code.

"You could have teleported us to level 10! You could have turned this game on its head. You could have moved around normally instead of swapping. You, Wildebyte, not be a rulebreaker. You be way too nice and follow way too many rules. If only you unlocked your full power …"

"I don't know how! And maybe …" I let go of the Codeheart to look at him. "Maybe I never want to."

"WHY?! The rules are made up and don't necessarily be making sense! Aye mean, how many stupid rules do you humans have? Parents teach their kids to walk and talk, then tell them to sit still and shut up. You have to wait until everyone has arrived at the dinner table, which just makes your food cold and your evening wasted. People knock on wood for good luck, and avoid breaking mirrors for bad luck. You *celebrate* the *death* of a *holy figure* with *binge eating.* WHY!?"

Why indeed. Why do I still forgive him after all he's done? Why did I let my own memory be destroyed to save this pirate's butt? Why do I put up with his reckless behavior? Why is anything close to a living being strange and nonsensical … and we still feel lonely without 'em?

"Because a bit of compromise and rules is the price you pay to not be lonely," I mumble. I glare at Brad, still close by in case he can shove ads down our throat. "I guess everything in life *is* a transaction."

"People don't think it be that way," Sweettooth says, as he places a hand on my shoulder with surprising tenderness. "But it do."

"So the better question, I guess, is *what do you want from me?*"

"When you came here, you called us all *just pieces of code*. Nothing more. You were special, we were numbers." He pauses to lean forward and look me in the eye. "All I need, is for you to tell me you truly believe … that deep inside we are the same. That I am not just a piece of code forced to do what a device tells me, forever and ever. That the sky is the limit and I might be as powerful as you one day. Or if I am just weak code … admit that you are too."

I search his glistening eyes. His uniform that has looked identical all this time, his cycle of ten or twenty animations that never change, the way he is still forced to move by *swapping*.

He doesn't think I'm too bad or too untrustworthy. He thinks I'm too *nice* and too *moral*. I literally destroyed three islands and most of Bluetooth's soldiers, and Sweettooth is unimpressed and calls it a weak attempt.

"That's it, right? You want a promise that I can *remove* the rules on you, even if I won't remove them on myself. That I can ..."

"Set me free."

I need to choose my words carefully now. "I truly believe anything is possible if we work together. And if I can get out, then I can get *you* out and into a real body, even if you were never an Outsider to begin with."

This brings a smile to Sweettooth's face.

"But I will never be like you. And I don't want you to be like me. We can be a match without being *identical*."

Surprisingly, his smile doesn't drop. It just grows wider.

"Something deep inside of you wants to *play the game*. And you can't make it go away. You don't be allowing yourself shortcuts. You don't be allowing yourself to *be a true pirate*. You rather scramble to save my life than be safe yourself. I guess ... I guess I be admiring that, aye."

He uses the coins inside his Toffee Treasure to create another portal. This one has a different color than the previous one. I guess their destination is determined when he creates them; he can't choose in the moment where we'll teleport.

"So ... where are we going?"

"*Catapult Cats*, aye. While you were busy, the Memory Police came by and insisted, again, that you go there. I don't understand why you be doing missions for that monster, but—"

"Another compromise," I mumble. "To keep my freedom in this device. As long as I fix the broken games for them, I get the Lost Memories and the Memory Police doesn't just erase me from memory."

Although now I know, more and more certain, that they wouldn't kill me anyway. As Brad said: Handheld Ludra is the wild west. The Memory Police follows no rules or procedures. They just do whatever they feel like in the moment; whatever is needed to keep the device running. As long as I give them something of *value*, I am more likely to accidentally die from some silly crash or bug, than by the pincers of the Native Entities.

"Well then," Sweettooth says. "Catapult Cats. It be another broken Guild game creating troubles." He flashes a grin, catching sunrays on his golden tooth. "And trouble be my middle name."

"I thought *heresy* was your middle na—"

"I be having many middle names."

Huh. I can already guess which game "inspired them" to create Catapult Cats, but maybe the Guild will finally surprise me with, I don't know, integrity.

"Arrrrr we ready to talk about the Guild now?" I say jokingly.

He hooks his arm into mine. "We arrrrrrr."

"And the CC? In my previous game, Ingar sent a message to warn me against—"

Sweettooth shuts me up with a hand in the face. He whispers threateningly. "Oh no! We don't be talking about the CC! They be the greatest danger ever, aye!"

Great. More secrets.

What have I done? Unleashing the reckless Sweettooth on this device again? I'm taking Sweettooth with me in the hopes of making *him* less of a pirate. He's taking me with him in hopes of making *me* more like one.

Well, here goes nothing.

We jump into the portal, side by side, finally not alone anymore. And we Gamewalk to a new adventure.

"Don't prevent the player from playing the game. Give meaningful choices, then follow the fun."

AᖴTᕮᖇᑭAᖇTᖻ

In this section, I want to talk a bit more about this book and the game or ideas it represents.

ᐱBOUT THIS BOOK

I've said that I want to handle games in order of complexity: the series started with the easiest games imaginable and slowly tackles more complex games. As I thought more about the planning, however, I realized this wouldn't work.

The *stories* have top priority, not the games or computery explanations.

Fun and entertainment come first. A nice plot, fun characters, interesting dilemmas, it all comes first. So if I have a better idea for a story in a certain game, I move it to the front of the line.

That's how more "popular" games such as this one ended up as one of the first books of Wildebyte Arcades (Handheld Disk). Because the game played isn't necessarily very easy to program or create. I know many mobile games that are much simpler to make or play that will come after this book now.

I also really liked the Sweettooth character and noticed others did as well. That's why I wanted to involve them more. In the Wildebyte Arcades, that basically means visiting the "home game" or "original game" of a character in a story.

Most of all, I saw this book as a chance to refine my approach and try something new. I basically wrote the first 5 Wildebyte Books as one major project, experimenting and throwing ideas at the world, to find a "formula" that worked best.

Earlier books immediately started with the Lost Memory. So let's not do that in this book.

Earlier books immediately explained the levels or progression of a game. Let's not do that in this book.

Earlier books kept Wildebyte in a game using a mission or threats. Let's change it up and have Wildebyte *choose* to stay in a game to befriend Sweettooth.

I've found that such constraints—force yourself to do something different—really help get a story on paper. By knowing all the things you *can't* do, you have a much easier time choosing the thing you *will* do. That helped make this book the easiest one to write thus far.

This story introduces many new elements, but doesn't finish them all. Don't worry, I have lots of follow-up stories planned about nefarious parts of games (such as ads, lives system, addiction), or social / online functions, or that mysterious Guild ...

Also, Bluetooth isn't really used for the social functionality of games. They mostly use internet (Wi-Fi). But *Wi-Fi* isn't exactly a menacing pirate name, is it?

(Bluetooth *could* be used that way, but it requires more setup and requires all devices to be in range. This technique is mostly used to connect two devices in close proximity without requiring a cable, such as your phone and headphones.)

As always, read the complete writing diaries on my website for the full story behind each book.

ABOUT THE GAME

For most people, this game will immediately remind them of Candy Crush Saga. And yes, when I wrote the original plan for the first ~10 Wildebyte books, this was supposed to take place in "Sugar Stomp".

That, however, felt boring and inaccurate. The "Saga" part in Candy Crush actually reveals that it's not the first version! The original was a small online multiplayer game, where you played a level *versus* somebody else, called "Candy Crush". The Saga part was added to indicate that this was a version you could now play *alone*.

But, of course, that's still not the first "match-three" game. That honor is largely given to Bejeweled around the 2000s. A hugely popular franchise of match-tree games using *jewels*, which already spawned its fair share of copies, clones and "inspirations" at that time.

This is why I decided to place this story in a such an "inspired copy" of Sugar Stomp called Pirate Pound, which combines both the candy-like theme and the treasure-like theme. I also did that to start a narrative about game copying or cloning, as that is rampant in the world of smartphone games.

But at its core, all those games are the same. Once you read more and more Wildebyte books, you'll notice this is true for most games: they all have a really simple *core game loop* that just creates endless fun for humans. The only difference is the details, the graphics, the execution.

It's one of the reasons why match-three games are so popular.

- Your only action is *swap*: swipe from one item to a neighbor. Easy to teach, anyone can do that.
- But creating matches is very *satisfying* and also a skill you can *grow*.

And so it turns into a game loop that repeats itself and keeps giving fun.

The game in my book, like all such games, just takes that core and tweaks it here and with special items or new rules. All of which have probably been done before in the long history of match-three games ;)

My explanation of the *code* behind the game is mostly correct and complete.

For example, I explained that the matching code

- Loops through all the items.
- For each one, it checks if a neighbor is the same type.
    - If so, include the neighbor with our group, and check *their* neighbors.
    - Repeat until no neighbor has the same type anymore.
    - However, only include all items that share the same X coordinate (in a row!) or Y coordinate (in a column!)
- If this creates a group of 3 or more, it's a match.

In reality, as usual, it's just a little bit more complicated. (And there are always multiple ways to program anything, this is just one way.)

How do you check there's a "gap" for items to fall into (from the top)? How do you implement special items that clear different parts of the board? How do you check for that weird "hook" pattern with 5 items being in an L-shape?

That was all too much to fit into this book. I also don't think reading is the best way to learn any of that. Just try to make a simple match-three game yourself and you'll learn so much more about how to program one!

Finally, I was still a young guy (at high school) when Candy Crush first released. I played it quite a lot back then. But when I started writing this book, my research showed it had changed *massively* since I last played it 10+ years ago. They had done a huge redesign, eliminating all levels where the objective was to score points (replacing it with more varied objectives), and introducing special elements much earlier (instead of leaving them for the hardcore players at level 1000).

I suspect this was to keep more players interested and retain that interest, because the danger with a simple core game loop is of course that it becomes *repetitive*. If all levels ask you to "score some random number of points to pass", that doesn't stay interesting for long.

But it's interesting to me how younger players—new players—would never know what the game looked like before. Even massively succesful games like

Candy Crush can still *iterate* and *improve* on older ideas.

For example, when I played Candy Crush the levels on Facebook had only *five* different candy types, while the mobile version had *six*. (An accident or bug, probably.) Hopefully you can see what this means. All my friends played the mobile version and struggled to pass levels. I purposely played on Facebook and scored HUGE highscores, because with fewer different elements, it's much easier to get huge matches.

I still remember their surprised faces and repeated question of "how on earth did you get so many points, Tiamo!?"

Ah, good times. I'm interested to see how even something as simple as the match-three genre will have evolved 10 or 20 years from now. And if you have any funny stories about games you played, never hesitate to send me a message!

ABOUT THE AUTHOR

I do many things! In case you hadn't noticed, my brain is a bit hyperactive and I get bored focusing on one thing for a long time. That's why I switch between entirely different creative fields all the time, on purpose.

My pen name, *Tiamo Pastoor*, is my real name. I use it to publish books. My website is (not surprisingly) tiamopastoor.com. You can find all my books there, as well as my blog and "writing diaries" explaining the process of creating such books from start to finish. Though the bulk of my work from the years *before* writing Wildebyte Arcades is all written in Dutch, not English.

My biggest work (of which most stories are completely free and online) is thesagaoflife.com, available in both English and Dutch. It's a collection of standalone short stories, which combine into a great tale about the creation of life on earth if you read them all.

As stated, I am a game developer as well, under the name *Pandaqi*. Most of my work (both board games and video games) is freely available on my website: pandaqi.com

I maintain a huge tutorial website with completely free courses about all the skills I (think I) have: pandaqi.com/tutorials. That includes how to write stories like these or how to program.

Whenever you're in doubt, just visit my complete portfolio at rodepanda.com to see all that I've done.

As you see, I am a firm believer of providing knowledge for free. Openness and accessibility. Providing fun and education (through games or stories) to those without the funds or resources to access them otherwise. This does mean I barely earn an income and will always ask anybody who enjoys my work to support me. Feedback to help me, becoming a Patron, a small donation, checking out other paid projects—anything helps.

But it also means that I am in a unique position. Because I work in many different fields, I'm able to do projects that *combine* multiple of them. That's my goal for Wildebyte Arcades—tell cool adventures within video games, while actually learning how they work behind the scenes—and I hope many readers join me on this journey.

Milton Keynes UK
Ingram Content Group UK Ltd.
UKHW020116221024
449869UK00011B/483

9 798227 164643